LAND OF NO DEATH

LAND OF NO DEATH

STANLEY ROBERTSON

BALNAIN

Published in 1993 by
Balnain Books
Druim House,
Lochloy Road,
Nairn IV12 5LF
Scotland

Typeset in Times New Roman
Printed in Britain by the Bath Press, Bath
Cover printed by Wood Westworth Ltd, Merseyside

British Library cataloguing-in-publication data:
A catalogue record for this book is avaliable from the British Library

Category: Fiction/Folklore

ISBN 1 872557 26 0

CONTENTS *page*

FOREWORD

The wealth of songs and stories lovingly preserved by the Scottish travelling people was revealed in the early 1950s with the discovery of 'folk champions' like the Stewarts of Blair and the matchless ballad singer Jeannie Robertson. A younger generation of traveller tradition bearers has since grown to maturity, and of these Jeannie's nephew Stanley is the acknowledged front-runner.

Inheriting a large part of his repertoire from the extended family of Stewarts and Robertsons, Stanley has increasingly displayed outstanding inventive talent of his own — particularly in the realm of story-telling, in which he has done effective 'missionary' work as far afield as Canada and the USA.

Stanley has shown himself to be an accomplished author and an outstanding 'folk hero'.

Hamish Henderson

Other titles by Stanley Robertson
(also from Balnain):
Exodus to Alford
Nyakim's Windows
Fish-Hooses
Fish-Hooses II

Cassettes:
Sangs and Ferlies (Birlers — Scotsoun)
Nippit Fit Clippit Fit (Aberdeen City Arts Dept)

to Mr and Mrs Albert Ydo of Leonen,
and Ben and Tina Lankeek, Holland

EVIL OMENS

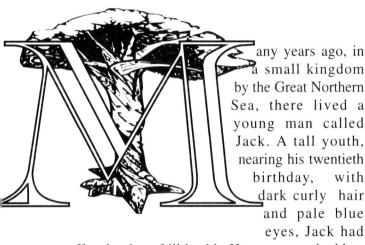

Many years ago, in a small kingdom by the Great Northern Sea, there lived a young man called Jack. A tall youth, nearing his twentieth birthday, with dark curly hair and pale blue eyes, Jack had never suffered a day of ill health. He was a good athlete and fishing, hunting and working the land were all part of his daily life. Jack had to support his aged mother and he knew what it was to work hard.

The village where he lived was right at the sea shore. His house was at the edge of the village, on the road to the market town, and every Friday, Jack would go to the market to trade and barter. He loved going there to meet friends and keep up with the news from all over the land. Often he found things to take home that he could not get in his own village.

On one particular day he was returning home from the market feeling pleased with himself. He had had an extremely good time trading for a milking cow. The sun was shining and Jack was in high spirits. Everything seemed to be going well for him.

All at once a beautiful magpie, with a long whirling tail, flew over his head and settled on a stone dyke near Jack.

'Good day!' it said.

Jack stood, amazed, but returned the greeting, 'Good day to you! Why do you greet me so politely? I can tell you aren't a bird of good omen.'

'I come with a warning, Jack, that you may be forearmed,' replied the magpie.

'Why should you give me warning? Why do you want to help a stranger?'

'Well, long long ago, when I was a fledgling, I fell off my nest. I would have been prey to foxes or weasels if it hadn't been for you, Jack. You came along and when you saw me on the ground, you picked me up and nestled me to your bosom and then took me up the tree to my nest again. I thought then, that if ever I could help you, Jack, then I would do so.'

Jack asked, 'But what is this message of warning you have for me?'

'Well, only the other day I was listening to my cousins, the crows, when I heard them say that their master, Death, was coming to place his hand on your head and was going to take you away! At least I can warn you!' And then the bird flew away.

Jack was very distressed by the magpie's news. Who would look after his aged mother or take care of the land

if he died? A thousand questions ran in his mind as he dragged himself home; his mood changed to despondency.

His mother saw immediately that something was very wrong, 'What ails ye, lad?'

Jack answered, 'Today a magpie told me that Death is coming after me, to lay his hand upon me and take me away.'

'Go at once to see your uncle Tom,' his mother replied, '— he'll tell you what to do!'

Jack ran straight away to Tom, the youngest of his uncles, to seek his advice. This uncle Tom was a jovial man, a blacksmith by trade. He fashioned all kinds of wrought iron work. Many a time Jack had been fishing with his uncle for they were good friends. The look on Jack's face shocked his uncle.

'Whatever's the matter?' shouted Tom.

'I've heard today from a magpie that Death is after me, to take me away,' Jack told him.

'Well, you're not without knowledge — I have taught you many things, and Death doesn't frighten me and nor does he look the road of me,' said Tom. 'So, I can promise that Death will not have the power to harm you, for I'll give you the protection of the trees: As long as the trees in the wood outside my garden have bark upon them, then Death shall not be able to touch you.'

Jack felt relieved. He knew that his uncle Tom had strange powers and if he said that Death could not touch him as long as there was bark on the trees, then he could believe him. He gave a great sigh of relief and shook his uncle's hand. He was ready to walk home to his mother's cottage, when down came many crows shrieking, 'You think that our Master, Death, doesn't know that you're being protected by the bark of the trees and the power of your uncle Tom! Well, Death has sent us here to start stripping the bark from all the trees in this wood!'

Once more, Jack's heart sank. What was he going to do now?

His uncle Tom scratched his head, 'This is as far as I can help you, Jack. You'd better go to see your uncle Dick, for he's wiser than I and will give you protection.'

Jack thanked his uncle Tom, for at least the crows couldn't strip the bark off the trees too quickly, though they started to peck and tear at little bits of the bark, he did have time. Jack raced to his uncle Dick's house.

Dick lived in a small cottage at the opposite end of the village from Tom. He was a quiet, wise man, who never engaged in idle gossip, indeed he seldom spoke, but when he did so every word was pure wisdom. Dick was a weaver and could produce the most intricate patterns upon his loom. Folks came from miles around to buy from him.

Jack was breathless, and his face worried, as he came into his uncle Dick's house. His uncle asked, 'What on earth is wrong with you today?'

Jack replied, 'I've been told that Death is coming to lay his hand upon me to take me away, and I don't know what to do! I went to uncle Tom, who gave me the protection of his trees, but Death knew what I was doing and sent crows to start stripping the bark from them.'

'Well, Jack! Death doesn't worry me nor does he look the road of me, so I'll give you my protection. I can tell you that Death has no power over you until that hill of gravel and sand in my back field is raised as flat as a pancake.'

If uncle Dick said that, then Jack knew it would be so,

for he had great powers. Jack gave a great sigh of relief, but just as Jack was leaving his uncle's house a great crowd of ravens came flying down, settling right in front of Dick's house.

One of the ravens spoke, 'You thought our master, Death, wouldn't know where you would go, but he did! He knew you would try to get protection here, so he's sent us to raise that hill of gravel and sand as flat as a pancake.'

Once more Jack felt terrible, for even though his uncle had given him a little more time in which to plan he felt hopeless. Dick called from his house, 'You'll now have to go to your uncle Gwillum, the eldest and wisest of us. I have taught you many things, so you're not without knowledge, but Gwillum will perhaps give you better protection from Death than we can, or else give you further instruction.'

Jack thanked Dick and sped off to his uncle Gwillum.

Gwillum's cottage lay right by the bay, where he had a small boat in which he liked to fish, though by trade he was a master carpenter. Gwillum possessed the white art, which he practised to help people in need. Jack loved his uncle Gwillum, who had taught him much. When Jack arrived his uncle welcomed him and poured him a glass of home-made berry wine. Jack was looking very distressed and Gwillum asked, 'Whatever's the matter with you? Why are your eyes so downcast?'

Once more Jack said, 'I've been told today that Death is coming to take me away with him!'

Gwillum answered, 'You are not without knowledge and I have taught you many things. Death doesn't bother me, Jack, because I've gained special knowledge and power, though I realise you don't have such powers yet.'

'But, uncle Gwillum, both Tom and Dick have given me the protection of the trees, and gravel and sand, which gives me a bit of time, yet I'm still worried.'

'Well, if your other uncles gave you that, then there's not very much I can add to help you.'

'But you're my last hope, uncle Gwillum. You must advise me what to do!'

Gwillum thought for a moment. Then he said: 'I believe you'll have to go to the Land of No Death.'

'The Land of No Death! — is there such place?'

'Indeed there is! But, although I can help you on the first part of your journey, you must follow my instructions to the letter, for they're very important.

'Tomorrow you must arise, long before the sun is up, and take a small sack of provisions to sustain you. Apart from food, water and wine, take a knife and make sure you get your mother's blessing. Then you must leave your mother's home and make your way here. Do not disturb me from my rest, but go to the beach outside. There you'll see a huge hessian sack. It will contain a few bones and things, but don't be concerned by them. Wait instead, until you see the sun just beginning to rise, then get into the sack and tie yourself inside it.'

Jack listened intently, because he knew that his life depended upon his uncle's instructions being obeyed in exact detail. Gwillum finished saying: 'You'd better go now to make ready for your long journey. One last caution I must give you — Beware the Dreaded Drunchan!'

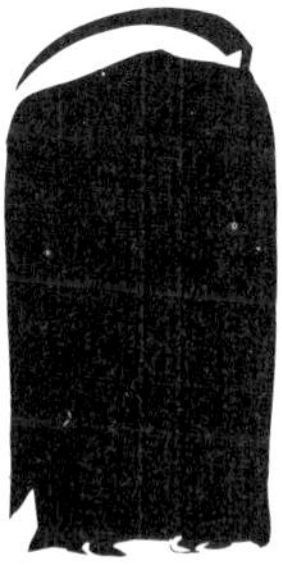

'What ever is the Dreaded Drunchan?'

'You'll find out soon enough. For now, understand that there are wizards abroad and you'll be tested and tried by many tasks before you truly find the Land of No Death.'

So Jack bade uncle Gwillum farewell and went home

to make preparations for his journey.

That night, Jack tossed and turned and could find little rest for thinking on the strange journey that he was about to make. In the early hours of the morning, Jack and his mother arose. She knew that her son had to make this journey, else Death would get hold of him. The old woman made him breakfast and put bread, wine and cheese in his sack. She gave him a mother's blessing and Jack was ready to begin the first part of his adventure. Jack told his mother how much he loved her and then added, 'Mother, should Death come looking for me at this house, then it's very important that you're prepared for his coming. Promise me that you'll not close your eyes if Death looks you in the face.'

His mother was surprised but gave him her word that she would obey him.

Jack left his mother's house and made his way to the sea shore, just below his uncle Gwillum's house. The sun was only minutes from rising as Jack took a long farewell look at his beautiful village. Then, just as the first rays of the sun came over the horizon, Jack climbed inside the hessian sack and tied himself in.

He was ready and waiting to begin the first part of his strange journey to find the Land of No Death...

THE DREADED DRUNCHAN

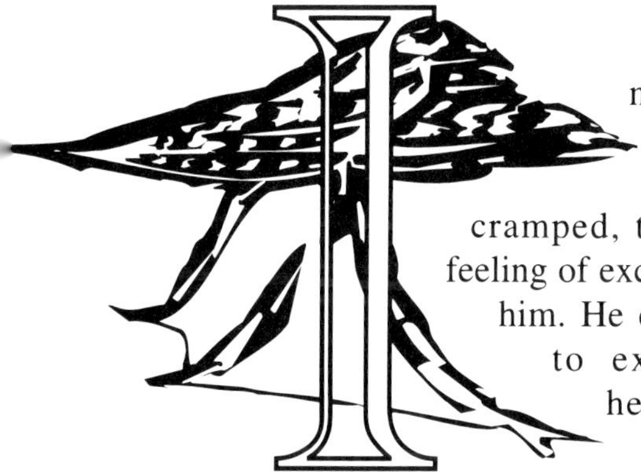

Inside the large hessian sack, Jack felt a bit cramped, though a strange feeling of excitement was upon him. He didn't know what to expect. Soon he heard the flapping of great wings of an enormous bird near him. With a sudden sweeping jerk, he felt himself being lifted off the ground and away into the heavens. The higher he went, the colder it became and Jack was glad of the provisions that his mother had put by for him. The journey turned out to be long and Jack grew weary. He could not see where he was going or in what direction he was being taken.

After what seemed like hours the great creature finally put him down. Jack cut himself free from the sack and caught only a glimpse of his carrier, a huge diamond eagle — the biggest he had ever seen, as it flew out into the night, leaving Jack at the top of a high mountain. Jack thought that it would be better to stay the night on this mountain and continue his journey in the morning

light, as it would be folly to try to find his way down in the dark. Jack lay down and covered himself over with the hessian sack. He was exhausted by the journey and soon fell asleep.

When the warm rays of the sun beamed down on Jack's face, he awoke to see a steep valley before him and, about five miles away, a small village. He wondered to himself if this might be the Land of No Death.

Climbing down the mountainside, Jack heard a terrible roar that sounded like a fierce lion.

Jack found himself confronted by a beast that looked like a man, but had the huge head of a dragon. It was growling and snarling. Jack remembered the story told by his uncle Tom of the Dreaded Drunchan. It was said that the monster was a wizard who had turned evil and taken on the shape of a man with a dragon's head. It would attack and kill anyone. Jack realised this would be a fearsome opponent, for the Dreaded Drunchan had the power to spit out fireballs. A touch from one was fatal, Jack remembered. If it could be disarmed however, then it was supposed to revert to a man once more. There was a chance that Jack might beat him in a fair fight. The beast growled, and its roar was frightening.

'You trespass on my land! I shall kill you!'

'Your mouth is bigger than your head!' Jack replied, 'and you'll have to catch me first!'

Jack said this to make the monster lose its temper. The Dreaded Drunchan hurled a great ball of fire at Jack's head, but it missed. The next fire ball went whizzing over Jack's head as he took cover behind a bush. Glancing down at the ground, Jack saw a stick, narrow at one end but thick and heavy at the bottom. It looked like the sticks that Jack and his uncle Tom used to play rock and caman with. Tom had taught Jack how to be an expert at that game. He grabbed hold of the stick and stepped boldly out in front of the monster. The Dreaded Drunchan began firing fireballs at Jack in rapid succession, while Jack responded, smacking every fireball back as quickly as the Drunchan could hurl them from his mouth. The monster had never seen such a master at this game, and it began to feel tired. He had lost energy and was beginning to weaken: the fireballs became smaller and slower, until only a few hot rocks came from his mouth. Jack was waiting for his chance to destroy the Dreaded Drunchan; only one more warm rock was fired. This was the moment Jack had anticipated, and he knew how to return this rock. It was perfectly aimed by the terrible Drunchan, straight at Jack's body, but Jack returned the rock right to the head of the beast. It hit its mark, the Dreaded Drunchan fell and Jack speedily went over, grabbed it by the neck and was about to insert his knife in its throat, when the monster pleaded for mercy and shrivelled into an ordinary man. 'Please! Spare my life! I give you my wizard's promise that I'll never terrorize another living soul.'

Now Jack knew that if a wizard gave his word then he would have to keep it: 'You will also promise that you'll never harm anyone who comes on this mountain, or indeed frighten anyone again. You should now protect the people of the village and become their friend instead of being a monster.'

The wizard gave his promise. He would never be the Dreaded Drunchan again, unless the village was being threatened. So, they both walked to the Drunchan's cave-home where he freed four maidens whom he had taken as prisoners. The maidens were overjoyed to be released and prepared to go back to their homes in the village.

Jack and the maidens climbed down to the village. Everyone was delighted by their return. They made Jack a hero, and gave him the very best of food and wine.

The news of Jack's battle with the Dreaded Drunchan spread far and wide until it came to be heard by the King, who sent a messenger with a letter inviting Jack to the palace.

The King's palace was magnificent. Jack was greeted by the head butler. 'We are very pleased to receive you, though I am afraid that the King cannot see you just yet. His majesty has heard of your battle with the Dreaded Drunchan and is most impressed with your deed for the King has need of a valiant man who will perform some tasks for him. We have been instructed to give you new clothes and plenty of good food and wine. If you accept the King's wish, then tomorrow I will instruct you on what his majesty would have you do.'

Jack was escorted that night to a room with beautiful furnishings. He slept well in the luxurious bed.

In the morning he arose refreshed and dressed himself in the fine clothes that the King had given him. He wanted very much to see the King but the butler came for him and told Jack that a small ship was waiting for him to take him away to where another young king was in need of help. On completion of the task required by this king, Jack was to ask for a ring, as a token that the task had been successfuly completed.

The butler added, 'I have given you a really good sailor as your helper on this voyage.'

A young lad of about fourteen then appeared and introduced himself as Bobbin. What a strange-looking lad he was! His hair was pure white and shone like a river. It seemed to move and shimmer like waves on an ocean. He had the largest green eyes Jack had ever seen and was dressed only in a pale blue shirt and short leather trousers. Jack felt a bit apprehensive taking a young lad on such a voyage. The butler saw the look of doubt in Jack's eyes and said: 'Bobbin was found in the sea when he was a baby. A woman who was gathering sticks on the sea shore rescued him. He has extraordinary senses and by smell alone knows the direction of any place sought. He can even navigate without the use of stars. There is no one in the land who can match his prowess in swimming, or stay underwater for so long. We think that because of his great abilities in these things he must be the child of one of the sea-kings, but up to now none has claimed him. He is called Bobbin because he is always in the sea and his head is always bobbing up and down. We assure you that he will be a great help to you.'

'And I can fish as well without needing rod or net,' Bobbin added.

Jack apologised to Bobbin, 'I am sorry for doubting your ability just because of your youth. I shall be most honoured to have you aboard as my friend.'

KINGDOM OF MARDARAS

The sea was as calm as a mirrored lake, while a gentle breeze caressed the sails of the little ship. Bobbin was indeed an excellent sailor and knew exactly in which direction to steer. Jack had plenty of worries on his mind. He thought about his own village and the events taking place there: was there still bark upon the trees, or gravel and sand upon the hill? And his mother who was still alone — could she manage on her own? Was she in danger from Death? Jack felt helpless being so far away.

This was their third day at sea and the voyage had been pleasant so far. Bobbin shouted suddenly: 'Land ahoy!' He pointed to the Island of Mardaras. Looking at the high, rocky shores of the island, Jack could see the famous palace of the young King. It was an impressive sight from the sea — standing right at the top of a hill, radiating a brilliant glow, like a pearl on a crown. Jack had always thought the palace to be dark, but now he could see for himself that it was white. They anchored the ship in an inland bay and the two lads made their way towards the palace. Mardaras was a beautiful and verdant place. The roadside was abloom with flowers and vegetation. Behind the palace huge forests could be seen. They walked up to the palace and were welcomed in.

Both were given new suits of clothes; Bobbin was

very reluctant to wear his. The young king was a tall man, with a regal air about him. He bid them welcome to his court and immediately began to tell Jack about the problem he had within his kingdom, while Jack and Bobbin listened attentively.

'As you're probably aware, there are many wizards abroad today and I think that I'm the victim of one such malicious wizard. I inherited my father's throne only a year ago and have tried to rule as wisely as I know how. My father was a good king, but he had many old-fashioned ways with him. He always kept the palace as dark as a dungeon for instance, it was always painted black: so dull and dowdy! So, as I've been to other lands and

seen the beautiful palaces that other kings live in, I said to myself that if ever I became king then I would change the whole place and have it brilliant white, with every part of it shining like a gem till it became famous, like a jewel in the world!

'And that's what I did, for as you can see I have created a beautiful palace. Now you would think that I would find joy in such wonderful surroundings, but I most certainly do not. Somehow, I think I've incurred the wrath of a wizard, perhaps through jealousy; while whoever it is, he's caused me such immense problems here that these past few months have been terrible for me and for my queen!'

'What's the nature of the terrible affliction caused by this wizard?' asked Jack.

'You'll find out for yourself, tonight!' replied the king.

The palace was a marvellous place: spiral marble columns; high, towering minarets; arrays of hanging flowers at the entrance to the first courtyard and, further inside, a great pool. It was just in front of this pool that the king kept court, and this was also where Jack and Bobbin were treated to a banquet, with dancing and singing. The young king told them that the island was theirs to roam about in with complete freedom, but they should be back at the palace before midnight.

Jack decided to have a walk up to the great forests, and Bobbin couldn't get out of his uncomfortable clothes quickly enough. Then he went to the seashore to be close to the sea.

As he walked along the shore, Bobbin met a very pretty girl with long dark hair who had just been swimming. She was a very pleasant girl and the two got on well right away. They swam together for a while and wandered about the sea shore. Then Bobbin remembered that he had to be back at the palace before midnight. So he took his leave of her, promising to meet her again soon.

As he entered the palace he met Jack returning from the forests. The king and queen were waiting for them: 'I am glad you are both happy here, for soon it will be the time for the great trouble to begin.'

They were right. A strange, weird flapping of wings could be heard, and guards and servants started running everywhere, looking for places to hide. Taking a large embroidered blanket, the king covered himself and his queen, while Bobbin said to Jack, 'Quick! I can sense danger; jump in the pool with me, we will be safe there.'

From the pool, they had only their heads above water to witness whatever was about to happen.

Suddenly, the whole palace was crawling with huge creatures like bats. They swamped the whole place, biting, clawing and tearing at everything and it was an awesome sight. To be without cover would be most dangerous. For about three hours this attack continued. When at last it stopped the servants had to clean up the whole palace. Jack and Bobbin took their places once more in front of the king, who now spoke: 'You have now experienced the calamity that attacks us every night. It must be the wicked spell of a wizard, who for some quite unknown reason, sends these bats of hell to torment me.'

But Jack said: 'There are no wicked spells, your majesty, just a little foolishness!

'Your noble father was indeed a wise man who learned much from your grandfather and his ancestors. Mardaras Palace was always famed for its beautiful location on top of this high rock. But it was also always known as a drab palace, where everything was painted gray and black. I know that it looks far better now than ever before, but I assure you that the true purpose for it being so drab in colour is due to the large sea caves that are full of those monster fruit-eating bats. As the palace is directly on their route to the fields and forests of their feeding grounds, the bats have to fly above here every night. When it was black, the bats always flew over the palace, but now it's a brilliant, radiant white it has become a great distraction to them. They become confused by the brilliance and so attack the palace every night.

'You, Sire, in your enthusiasm thought to make sweeping changes within the palace, but the result is drastic. Forgive me for speaking plainly.'

Feeling somewhat stupid, the king shook his head. 'Jack, I admire your candid speech, for now I see how foolish I've been, thinking to reject the ways of my forefathers.'

So the king set all the people from the palace and round about to start painting everything in drab colours, so as not to attract the bats anymore.

The following night the bats did not return! The king was overjoyed, for it was far better to live in a dull palace than to be eaten by bats every night! Jack was given a ring with a red stone on it to take back to the mysterious king, so as to prove the task had been completed.

The lads stayed a couple of days on the island at the king's pleasure, but Jack knew how imperative it was to get away and continue his quest for the Land of No Death.

Bobbin was sad to have to leave the beautiful girl, who was so much like him in nature. Her name was Maera and Bobbin promised to return to see her. He waved goodbye and headed for the ship, where Jack had already made everything ready in his haste to depart.

They returned to the King, though his butler relayed the news that he could not see them until all the tasks were finished. The ring with the red stone was handed over to be given to the King.

Their next trip was to take place within a few days, after they were sufficiently rested. Jack had to explain to the butler that he could not wait because of his personal plight. Bobbin agreed, suggesting that they could rest on the ship. So the butler asked them to stop for one night while the ship was filled with more provisions and fresh water, and told them that on the morrow their journey would take them to the Island of Horgan, where another young ruler was in need of help.

Jack went to bed that night with his mind sorely troubled by thoughts of his mother and uncles. He wondered again whether Death had visited his mother's home...

He was now obsessed with trying to find this strange place — The Land of No Death

SEA-KELPIES

The voyage to the Island of Horgan proved to be a dangerous one. They set out with dark and overcast skies and all the signs of a terrible storm.

Bobbin voiced his fears to Jack. 'I'm worried that we may be embarking on this voyage to Horgan at the start of bad weather. It looks as though it'll be a difficult trip for us.'

'I know it would be better to wait,' replied Jack. 'But I don't have the time to spare. The old enemy is against us and we have no other choice but to brave it out and hope that we can get there in safety.'

'I fear no weather — that's always been my motto!' laughed Bobbin. And so they set off.

They had been at sea for barely an hour when the most awful tempest arose and great thundering waves pounded the sides of the little ship. It became so bad that Jack had to tie himself against a mast, while Bobbin plodded on attending to what needed doing. The storm continued for days. They were at the mercy of the elements.

Eventually, on the fourth day, it settled and Jack and Bobbin found themselves on a quiet shallow sea, near a huge cave. They had been blown miles off their course for Horgan, but they were glad to be alive. Now there was not as much as a breeze to sail by.

The ship did not seem to be in their control but at the mercy of providence and the elements.

The sun beat down mercilessly for two days. To save themselves from being burned, they had to take cover by going below deck or else staying in the sea. Bobbin loved being in the water. Jack occasionally went into the sea but the currents were very strong for him, even though the water was shallow and barely reached two fathoms. There was a large cave nearby, but experience had taught them both that it was dangerous to go exploring into hidden unknown realms unless essential, so both the lads kept away.

On the third day, Bobbin was down below in the galley preparing some salads and sea fruits for them to eat, whilst Jack gently floated on top of the shallow sea immediately off the stern side of the ship. He was holding a rope in his hand in case of drifting away too far from the ship, while his mind crammed itself with worries about the safety of his family back home. He did not hear a sea kelpie approaching him. It came nearer and nearer. Unknown to Jack, the cave that they had moored so close to was the home for many sea kelpies. With webbed feet and sharp claws on their hands, these creatures resemble rather purplish human beings but for the scales all over them. Their razor-sharp teeth, like sharks, had claimed many a mariner.

This sea kelpie came right up to Jack, grabbed him by

the waist and swam with him back to the cave. Jack struggled, but it was all in vain as the sea kelpie was so much more powerful.

Bobbin came up on deck just then with the food, and he caught a glimpse of the sea kelpie carrying Jack into the

cave. Bobbin threw down the tray of food at once and ran for a gong hanging on the side of the cabin. Grabbing the gong, he jumped into the water and started banging it furiously.

Within moments dolphins appeared, seeming to understand what Bobbin was doing, for he then climbed on board again and this time he threw down ropes, looping them round the bodies of the dolphins. He tied the other ends to the ship and then hastily got hold of the oil lamp and a small mirror and dived once more into the water making this time for the sea kelpies' cave.

At the entrance to the cave he grabbed bunches of dried seaweed, smashed the oil lamp and, covering it with the seaweed he used the mirror to concentrate the sun's rays on the heap which burst suddenly into flame. As soon as it started burning well, Bobbin covered it with damp seaweed and great gulches of thick black smoke billowed into the cave. Bobbin then moved inside the cave and saw that it was littered with bones, the remains of sailors that had fallen foul of the sea kelpies.

The smoke was following Bobbin thickly. Inside the main part of the cave it was very dark, but he could see the kelpies in the gloom. They had placed Jack on a deep tubbed table, filled with stinging blue jellyfish and Jack was shouting in agony from the pain of their stinging. As he drew near, Bobbin screamed out, and the sea kelpies turned round to see who the intruder was. They were blinded momentarily by Bobbin's glowing white hair. Gulches of the smoke filled the cave and in the choking confusion, Bobbin went straight to the table and grabbed at Jack. In spite of being in great pain, Jack managed to hold on to Bobbin as he ran and then swam madly back to the safety of the ship, where instantly Bobbin gave orders to his friends the dolphins, who started pulling the ship away from the area.

The dolphins pulled the ship away for nearly three miles, until they were safe from the sea kelpies. Bobbin thanked the dolphins, who swam happily away. Next, he dived into the sea to gather special sea herbs with which to make an antidote for the poison of the jelly-fish stings. Once the herbs were rubbed into the stinging wounds and a cup of fresh jelly-fish tea had been administered to Jack, the pain from the stings began to subside. It took another day before Jack was well enough to continue the voyage — and that was another day of time lost.

The elements took pity on them, and soon a prevailing wind filled their sails and they were able to get under way again.

It was two days later when Bobbin shouted: 'Land ahoy!'

There on the horizon were the mountains and cliffs of Horgan. What new adventure lay in store for them there?

ISLE OF HORGAN

Horgan was a stony island with some fertile land on one side. The palace, perched on a polished rock, was built of marble and was beautiful to behold. Horgan was not a large kingdom and was administered by a young ruler called Yorgo. Jack knew nothing about him. The two lads wondered what it was they would be required to do in this place as they guided their ship into the small rocky harbour, and then walked the mile towards the imposing palace.

Strangely, there were no people to welcome them. Instead they were given a cold reception at the palace by King Yorgo, an arrogant, proud man. There was an air of haughtiness about him and he offered no refreshment or change of attire to his new guests. Standing beside the monarch was a tall, lean, fellow with a strange-looking smile that seemed to be almost a sneer.

Jack asked the king how he might be of help to which the king replied, 'I do not really need any help from anyone, as my councillor here, the Wizard of Horgan, can do everything for me.'

Surely this cannot be the famous Wizard of Horgan Jack wondered, for he remembered long ago hearing about the Wizard of Horgan from his uncles, who had said that the Wizard was a very ancient man. Here however was a comparatively young one. So Jack said, 'I have heard of your great feats of magic, your reputation is revered by all.'

'Oh, no!' said the young King Yorgo. 'This is my new wizard whom I have called here to help rule my kingdom. The other one was the wizard my father used. He proved treacherous, so I banished him to the other side of the island. Indeed, it was kind of me not to take his life and I spared him only because of his faithful service to my father. But, when my father died, I could get no peace to rule from that interfering old man. Then I met this far better and younger wizard whom I now trust completely, indeed he has been a blessing to me. He has helped me in everything I have done concerning the kingdom.

'Recently, however, that evil old Wizard of Horgan has put a hex or a spell on me, which means that every day now I must leave the palace for about four hours and be forced to go with my people into a huge rocky cave near the shore. I don't know truly what happens meanwhile, but I do know that if I don't do this then my people and I will perish. My wizard here tells me that deadly vapours come down and for this evil, the old Wizard of Horgan will surely be put to death. You and your friend will have to find a way to stop this evil spell, and instead of coming to the cave with us, you will have to remain here to find out what happens. The only person who can withstand the vapours is my new wizard, who has been trying hard to break the spell. As he doesn't yet know the magic connected with it, he's still trying to find the solution.'

'What time of day does this thing take place?' asked Jack.

'It starts in the late afternoon and finishes by early evening,' answered the king.

'Good. Then that will just give me time to try and see the old Wizard at his work and perhaps understand a bit about the nature of the spell. If we go now then we can reach the wizard before the vapours start.'

The king granted the two friends leave and retired to a room in the palace. Jack and Bobbin went outside and made tracks for the other side of the island to find the old Wizard. 'I don't like the look of that young wizard,' said Bobbin, 'I think he knows more than he tells the king.'

'And I don't understand why the old Wizard would change his ways after serving the old king for so long a time,' said Jack. 'But never mind, we'll find out the strange going's-on in this place, even though it may be the last thing we ever do!'

They climbed over a high hill to the other side of the island where they looked out for the home of the old wizard. Away down a lonely valley they could see an old hovel of a house. As the two lads went towards it, Jack said to Bobbin, 'We'd better be careful, just in case the Wizard spots us and casts some kind of spell on us.'

Slowly and cautiously therefore, they sneaked over to the wizard's window and tried to see what the he was

doing. To their surprise, the Wizard shouted: 'Jack and Bobbin, you'd better come in and speak to me!' When they entered his cottage, the Wizard had a meal waiting for them!

'You don't have to be afraid of me,' said the old man, 'if I wanted to harm you folks, then I'd have hurt you while you were still at sea. Since young King Yorgo didn't have the manners to feed you I took it upon myself to make you a meal.' Now although the outside of the house looked a terrible hovel, the inside was clean and tidy.

Jack asked, 'Why did you cast a spell on the king and quarrel with him?'

The Wizard replied, 'I only wanted to show him the folly of his ways and try to steer him in the right direction. He's an arrogant young man and seeks to do everything in a new fashion although the tried and tested ways are correct. Many an anxious hour his father and I used to have about him, but at least the old king always took counsel and we got on well together. He was a wise man, but unfortunately, his successor is still very foolish. Another person now has the ear of the king, who cannot see past him. He flatters him all the time, and I fear he has a motive. I tried to warn the king about him, but he thought I must be the evil one and now am banished. I have never done anything to harm the ruler, nor indeed the realm of Horgan.'

'Then who is this new Wizard of Horgan?' asked Bobbin.

'He is not human at all. He is Boorg, a subman from the caves away underneath the earth. The submen are half-animal, half-ape. Long ago there was a great war between the submen and man. The humans won whilst the submen went to live under ground. There have been many years of peace between the two groups, although now the evil Boorg wants to claim the Realm of Horgan, make himself monarch and rule both the humans and submen. I know of this evil plan but, being a wizard, I am bound by certain rules of conduct. This means that I am not allowed to stop his evil spell — still, I can give you help to do your best to stop him.'

'Will you please give us as much information as you can about the situation, so we can be forearmed?' asked Jack.

'Yes, but firstly, you must understand that it's not my spell, though I can tell you what you can do to stop it. Every day, at the same time, there is a eruption of sulphur and boiling lava, which issue from a small mound near the palace. These eruptions give off the dreadful poisonous fumes which cause the people to go into hiding.

The evil Boorg has a wicked scheme that comes into operation today after the mound bursts. You see, there is a secret passage-way from the world of the submen that goes right into the palace. Today, while the king and all his committees are hiding in the caves, Boorg means to have all the submen come up to earth where they can capture the humans and enslave and exile them to the submen's world. Meanwhile he will take over the kingdom of Horgan.

You lads have a couple of hours yet to put a plan of mine into action. If you're succesful in your part then I will return to the palace and explain the whole affair to the king, who I hope will have come to his senses.

'These then are my instructions to you. As you're the

elder of the two, you must fight Boorg and win. To you and everyone else he's a man, but really, he is not, he only uses the facade. It is but a body mask. Boorg wears a jewelled snake bracelet upon his right arm and that's what gives him cover from what he really is. If you can take the bracelet off his arm he will then revert to the appearance of the subman. That then is your task.

'Now, Bobbin. You will have to go to the sea and wait there until just before the mound erupts. I'll give you long pipes of strong reed, which you must join together and make into one huge pipe. Then you'll have to take one end into the sea and get the sea-water to flow through it and insert the other end into the erupting mound of earth. The volume of the sea water will drown the force of the poisonous flow from the mound. This will cause many problems for the submen and should stop them from completing their plan. Boorg meanwhile should be in the palace, waiting for the arrival of his men from below, whom Bobbin will have stopped in their tracks.

'Now, to you again Jack. You must go to the palace unseen and somehow catch Boorg unawares, in order to take off his bracelet and expose him for the evil subman he is. You cannot go by the road, as Boorg is waiting for you, but must take instead the road through the land of submen. Bobbin may take the ordinary road back over the hill to the sea, because by the time he returns everyone will be going into the cave. He will have to work fast — for it's essential to have your timing perfect.

'Jack — you must take the trap-door underneath this cottage and sneak through the land of the submen. They'll kill you if they catch you. The road goes straight to the palace, although there are many devious roads leading off it. On no account take any other road than the straight course. It is very dark down there, so I'll give you a small lamp. Keep it under your jacket. I know it will be difficult for you to see, but I have nothing else I can give you at this time. You'll have to take extra caution, but remember — there are many people who will be depending on you both to complete your tasks.'

The Wizard then gave them both his blessing and the two lads made their separate ways to their tasks as they had been advised.

Bobbin ran like the wind over the hill, making his way toward the shore. He could see in the distance many people going into the cave and taking their animals with them.

Meanwhile, Jack went down through a trap-door, down to the road that went deep into the submens world...

Although Jack had the shorter route, it was a far more dangerous one. Down below him he could hear strange chants from the submen and there was a horrible smell of decayed flesh everywhere; he knew that if he was caught he would surely be murdered, so he hurried along the dark straight road, off which many others led. Sometimes Jack would start to go in the wrong direction, but he always checked himself quickly. He wished Bobbin was with him, because Bobbin always knew the direction, but Jack knew that he too would be racing against time — trying to fix the reed hose together to reach from the sea to the mound before it exploded...

And Bobbin was indeed at the sea. His hands were sore tying the pieces of the reeds together. He worked against time, until it was finished and placing one end in the sea, with the other he ran to the mound. To his horror he realised the reed pipe was about ten feet short. This was fatal! Bobbin ran like a hare to the sea and dived in. There were reeds there that were suitable, but they lay very deep down. Bobbin summoned all his energy. He struggled to gather the reeds and seaweed to bind them, before the submen surfaced to raid the palace...

Meanwhile Jack was making good time. He sensed the submen close by, making for the palace. Jack was about a hundred yards in front of a crowd of them. His only problems were not to get lost and to keep ahead of the submen. At long last, Jack came to the end of the path and fumbled for the trap-door that would take him into the palace. He could hear the submen coming fast upon his heels and with the submen only a few yards behind emerged from the passage. Jack sat down hard upon the trap-door to try to keep them below, hoping very much that Bobbin had completed his side of the task!

Boorg was in the state room, dressed up in the robes of office and wearing the crown of Horgan. He thought his scheme was well and truly complete and was just waiting for his submen to come into the palace, from where they would capture all the humans and take them prisoner.

Quickly, Bobbin tied the last pieces of reed together and the water started to flow. With much difficulty, he managed finally to get the end of the pipe into the earth mound. It was but seconds away from erupting and putting out poisonous fumes of sulphur. Now the sea-water cascaded down the pipes gaining momentum and the great force started to flood the submen. They panicked, fleeing down to their homes in the depths of the earth. They would be safe there, but their routes up to the earth would now be destroyed.

Bobbin had achieved his part of the task. Now it was left to Jack to fufil his. He could hear the water below gushing and gurgling and so he knew that the submen would start home for safety before they drowned. It was important now that Boorg be fought, in order to show the king the foolishness of his ways and in the hope that the old wizard would be reinstated to his position as councillor to the king.

Boorg was sitting in state, waiting for his men and thinking the crown was safely his. Jack quietly sneaked right up behind him. Surprise would be the element that Jack would have to use. With all his strength, Jack suddenly grabbed Boorg from behind. Boorg was so stunned by such an attack he did not know how to respond. Jack took advantage of his sudden shock and tore the snake bracelet from Boorg's arm. Immediately, Boorg turned into his own form as a subman and screamed like an animal at Jack.

'You poor human fool! Do you not know that I am ruler here now? All the humans on this island are now my slaves!' Boorg could see that this was a powerful man and he was himself really a great coward without his magic tricks to help him. To get Jack onto his side he said, 'Man, I like your courage! If you remain here as my advisor then, I promise, I'll make you a really powerful man!'

Jack was not one for being bought and he was even more surprised that the subman would not fight him. It was then he realised that Boorg was a great coward, who even though he could be much stronger than Jack, did not have the bravado that Jack or Bobbin had, for they were truly courageous and believed in truth and right. But Boorg hid behind a cloak of deceit.

When the time was up for the young king and his people to come out of the cave, the king was most surprised to see Jack holding a subman wearing the robes of power! The king shouted angrily, 'How dare a subman wear my clothes of office! Who are you and how did you manage to get into my palace?'

'By your leave, your honour, you invited him into the palace!' cried Jack.

'I am not so stupid as to bring a subman into the royal palace — what are you saying?'

'I am afraid you did, sire. This subman is Boorg, an evil wizard of the underworld whom you made your councillor. He was the one behind the evil spell. It was not the kindly old Wizard of Horgan. The old wizard has been the hero of this battle, not me. He knew all about Boorg's intentions and though he tried to tell you, you banished him to the other side of the island to live in a hovel after all those years of faithful service to your father.'

The king felt a fool. Jack gave him the snake bracelet that Boorg had used to make his deception. He was very angry and wanted to have Boorg executed immediately. But Jack told him to wait until the old wizard returned and to follow his advice. The king agreed and so the old wizard returned and was reinstated as the Wizard of Horgan.

The old wizard told the king, 'Boorg has been evil and is deserving of death, yet we must take into consideration that he is not human. Therefore he cannot be tried as a traitor, because he owes no loyalty to the state. He has tricked you and this crime should be punished. I would therefore ask, sire, that you spare his miserable life and banish him to the other side of the island as I was. Give me the snake bracelet, if you please, and I shall use it as part of my office, for I know how it works.' The king agreed, Boorg was banished to the lonely side of Horgan and the wise old wizard took his rightful place as councillor.

The king asked what reward Jack would like. Jack replied that if he could have a ring with which he could return to the other land, this would be his second task completed. And so the king gave Jack a ring with a blue stone in it and he gave Bobbin a medal for bravery. Bobbin was over the moon with that!

Jack and Bobbin were invited to stay at the king's pleasure for a few days, but the old wizard told them all that Jack must leave on the morrow, for he had more tasks to complete and time was now essential to him.

Peace and happiness returned to Horgan and the king, along with the wizard, waved adieu from the shore.

On the voyage home, Jack was troubled with thoughts of his own village. How happy he had been there. Now he was a vagabond without a true country. What more adventures would he have to encounter before completing the tasks for the mysterious king and before finding the Land of No Death that his Uncle Gwillum had told him about?

At least Jack had a true friend in Bobbin, with whom to share his travels.

THE SLINKERS

The voyage back from Horgan was pleasant and they were made welcome once more by the mysterious king's butler. A banquet was spread for them, which they enjoyed, yet Jack told the butler that he could not stay long and they planned to sail on the morning tide to wherever it was that the king would have them go.

Early next morning, the two lads made ready to sail again and awaited the king's instructions. The butler came down to see them.

'The king is very pleased with the success you've had in helping these rulers find solutions to their problems. He's sorry that he cannot greet you formally and sends his deepest regards to you both. He would now like the pair of you to sail for the Island of Gumboria, where yet another young ruler is in need of your services and should you complete this last task, then he will be most happy. If you can prove yourself worthy in this final voyage, then he can entrust you with his very own life. For the king has much need of a brave man and a wise one, who can solve his problems. I'll tell you more of this when you return again with the last ring.'

As Bobbin set sail for the Island of Gumboria, fair winds filled their sails. The journey seemed to be going very smoothly, yet Jack felt a strange uneasiness about this trip... Bobbin was delighted with the conditions at sea and there was a care-free atmosphere about him. He laughed at Jack for being so strangely glum, when everything was going so well for them and Gumboria was only two days journey away.

Now the great barrel of fresh water that Bobbin had filled personally for the journey was leaking, though nobody had yet noticed it. It had been harnessed onto the side of the bulwarks, but somehow a large nail had pierced it and the precious fresh water had started to dribble away in drops, which later became a fast flow. It went unseen, however, and only came to light when Bobbin went to take a drink and found that there was but a trickle in the barrel. This placed them in a very dangerous position. Bobbin informed Jack, who decided that they would have to stop at some nearby island to replenish the barrel. From the crow's nest Bobbin could see a small island, away in the distance to starboard, so they set sail for that. Jack still had this feeling of unrest within him... Could this be Death putting stumbling blocks before him, or was it an accident that the water barrel was pierced?

As they neared the island, Bobbin noticed that the sea had become very shallow and they decided to put down anchor before going any closer. The water was only two fathoms deep here and he couldn't risk placing the ship in peril.

'We can easily swim ashore from here and get some fresh water from a stream,' Jack decided. So, taking some containers, they both dived into the sea and swam for the island. It seemed barren where they came ashore, but on climbing into the hills they found it a very fertile place. There were a number of rivers and streams flowing with coloured water. Jack thought the one with a slightly reddish tinge would probably be best, he tried a little and said it tasted like fine wine! They sampled just a handful each and waited to see if it was poisonous, until after about ten minutes they knew it was quite safe in spite of its colour. They were both thirsty by now and

each drank a large amount. As they were about to fill their containers they grew very sleepy, and in no time were both sound asleep on top of the hills from where the red river flowed.

It was a very deep sleep and they both slept for many hours.

When Jack awoke, he found himself lying in a dark, damp prison! He shouted out, 'Where are we? How did we arrive here?'

A gruff, booming voice growled back, 'Since you intruded into the privacy of our island, you're going to be sold as slaves.'

Bobbin then rose up, rubbing his eyes drowsily and asking, 'What place is this?'

The booming voice growled, 'This is the Island of Slinkers.'

Jack and Bobbin looked toward each other in the dark and realised that they had been drugged by the waters of the red river. When they got to their feet and looked through a tiny hole

in the wall, they saw a large crowd of these Slinkers gathering.

The Slinkers were a tall, slender people, with scaly, reptilian features. By nature they were a close people amongst themselves, but hostile to strangers. The two lads were to be the great feature of their sale today, for non-Slinkers were of great value.

The gruff Slinker tied the lads together and took them out to a platform in the centre of town. These tall people gasped with delight when they walked onto the platform. First Jack was untied and paraded before the Slinkers, while a great furore arose from the crowd.

'We have before us a wonderful specimen of Man, who seems to be trained for work. He is strong and exceptionaly ugly, so we shall start the bidding at fifty Bluchers. Do I hear fifty Bluchers for this fine specimen?' The auctioneer was then kept busy as hands were raised in bidding for Jack. He was eventually sold to a rather cruel looking Slinker for three hundred Bluchers.

Jack was tethered again and bundled onto the back of a horse and cart to be taken away by the cruel-faced Slinker. The last that Bobbin could see of Jack was of him being hit with a stick by the Slinker as he watched the cart disappear over the hill.

There was a fifteen minute pause between the sale of Jack and Bobbin and as he was being untied, Bobbin noticed a grand coach coming in and a tall, regal lady Slinker came out. As she saw Bobbin she shrieked with delight: 'A perfect gift for my daughter's birthday! Little Balena will be delighted with that young toy!'

Bobbin's hair started to shimmer and move in rage, much to the delight of this lady Slinker, who happened to be the queen of all the Slinker race and to whom he was sold for only forty Bluchers, because he was so much younger and smaller than Jack. Poor Bobbin was about to be tethered again when the queen insisted that the boy was not to be tied up. Instead, she took him by the hand and led him into her grand coach and away to her wonderful palace — where she had him clothed in beautiful silks and satins and a fancy turban — for he was to be a special gift to the little princess. This was all much to the dismay and disgust of Bobbin, who was appalled at having to wear such terrible clothes. He was happy in his own clothes and really, he never changed them. Still, at least he was not being beaten or hurt by his owner. Little Balena was thrilled with Bobbin and amazed when his hair moved, which always occured when Bobbin was annoyed, or felt excited.

The queen was kind to him and treated him more like a son than a slave, for he presented no obvious threat to the Slinkers. He was not restrained from going out into the town at any time and nor were the Slinkers unkind to him. Everyone called him by name and he made friends everywhere he went. He hoped to use this to gain the full confidence of the queen and thus try to get Jack released.

Meantime, Jack was taken to an old mill, where he was harnessed onto a huge grindstone wheel, and made to turn it to grind the corn. It was a slow and painful task.

There was another young man in the mill also, who had to take his turn at the wheel of the grindstone. He told Jack that he was a shipwrecked sailor named Zac. He had managed to swim to shelter on this island, but he had been immediately seized and, like Jack, had been sold as a slave to work in this awful mill. The work was hard; the Slinker who bought them beat them with a stick if they slackened in any way. Jack was trying desperately to muster a plan of escape from this island, in which he could take Zac with him. It would have to be a faultless plan and they would need time to find Bobbin and then swim back to the ship. He was worried about his dear friend Bobbin, and knew that the longer he waited the weaker he would grow. So he decided that he needed to come up with a solution to be free of this island within a week. He was also in a desperate state because of his plight against Death, and he did not have time to waste working at the grindstone...

Now, Zac was weak and so Jack knew that any plan of escape would not only be difficult, but it would have to be successful in the first attempt.

Zac told Jack an amazing feature of the Slinkers — they could not swim. This was one of the reasons they mistrusted men, for they imagined that men were only interested in their treasures, of which the most valuable were their sea-shells. Brave Slinkers might go right near the water's edge to gather the shells, but they had a dreadful fear of the sea and not one of them could swim. If Jack and his fellow prisoner could therefore get to the sea, then they should be safe. But there was still Bobbin, who Jack thought must be imprisoned like they were, and there seemed no way of finding out where he was.

Near the palace of the Slinker Queen, there was a deep, walled hole in the ground. It was one of the most frightening places in the Isle of Slinkers because it went deep into the earth and the weird noises that came from it were supposed to be made by a sea-demon. Growls and snarls could be heard from the mouth at the top of the hole and this put the fear of death into the hearts of the

Slinkers. One or two brave ones would venture near the hole, but took great care not to fall in. This was the reason for the wall round it.

One day Bobbin walked by this hole and was not in the least bit afraid to look down into it. As he listened to the sounds coming from it, he seemed to recognize them. By putting his ear right over the hole he could definitely hear the sound of water. The mouth of the hole was not wide, but it was too deep and too dark to see the bottom. Bobbin dropped a stone into the gaping mouth and counted to eleven, so he knew it was about fifty feet deep. It could perhaps be a means of escape — yet it might also be a death-trap! Bobbin was worried now about Jack and wanted to discover where he might be, so he asked the queen's permission to find him. She agreed, and so eventually he found the mill, where the Slinker-in-charge allowed him a few minutes with Jack.

There was great joy on Jack's face when he saw Bobbin. They spoke hurriedly of escape to the ship. Between them, they plotted an escape for late that evening, and Jack introduced Zac into this plan. Bobbin would sneak out at night, when everyone was asleep and drug their guard.

During that evening, Bobbin went for a short walk down beside the mouth of the great hole and, though he was not aware of it, he was followed by little Princess Balena. The Queen, noticing that Balena was gone from her room, ran out after her daughter.

Bobbin walked over to the great hole to see if this might be a means of escape, for he knew that the Slinkers were very much afraid of it. Now Balena liked to be with Bobbin and so she came up behind him, right to the mouth of the great hole, where she slowly clambered onto the little wall surrounding the mouth. Bobbin, deep in thought, didn't notice Balena, but the queen who had been following, let out a scream as she saw her daughter climbing onto the wall of the dangerous place. Balena, startled by the scream, lost her balance and fell forward into the cavernous mouth of the hole of the sea-demon. The scream also alerted Bobbin, who without thinking, dived after Balena and they both fell a long way down into a deep pool of water. There, seeing the little girl struggling, he caught her and pulled her onto a dry shelf of rock nearby. Deep down in this peculiar place it was strangely light and Bobbin could see, clear as crystal, the large entrance of a sea-inlet. Within the cave there were a few sea-lions that panicked on seeing them and fled from the place back to the open sea. Obviously, it was a place of shelter for sea-lions when predators chased them, for they could come right into the cave and be safe from any sharks close to the shore. Also, though it seemed quite safe and harmless down here, the sounds of the sea-lions were distorted by the narrow tunnel into a weird noise like some kind of sea-demon. Bobbin now recognised the familiar sound that he had heard. Bobbin took the hands of the frightened princess and assured her that she was safe and that he would now take her back to her palace, where she belonged.

Meanwhile above the cave, the people were wailing about the loss of little Balena. The queen had fainted and had to be carried back to the palace, while all the other Slinkers were in deep mourning at the thought of the little princess being eaten by the sea-demon. The whole palace was in despair.

In about half an hour however, a slinker guard came screaming into to the palace: 'A miracle! A miracle!'

Everyone there came out to see what had happened and to their utter astonishment they saw Bobbin carrying little Balena, having escaped from the cave.

The queen wept with joy and ran to kiss her daughter and hug Bobbin. Mirth and laughter returned to the palace and the queen asked Bobbin: 'What is it that your heart would most desire?'

Bobbin seized the opportunity to have Jack and Zac released.

'I would like most of all, your Majesty, to have the release from captivity of my two friends, who are being kept at work on the mill grindstone.'

'Then if this is your desire, so let it be granted by royal decree! Let payment be made also to the Slinker that bought your friends, so that he shall not be impoverished.'

Bobbin was delighted when Jack and Zac were immediately released, only minutes before they were going to try to escape. How grateful they were to Bobbin for his great courage as well as his skill in swimming!

The queen asked Bobbin if he would be willing to teach some of the Slinkers to swim, for nobody on the island could do so, as they were all so afraid of water. Bobbin stressed to the queen that time was very precious to them, but he would teach some of the younger ones to swim. Next morning, Bobbin, Jack, and Zac taught the Slinker children to swim and they learned very quickly. Some of the adults learned to overcome their fear of water too. This new development of swimming seemed to strengthen a bond between the two races, creating a new trust. The Slinkers, who were not really a bad race, resolved to be friends with these men from other islands.

Bobbin asked to leave with his friends, to continue their journey to the Isle of Gumboria, where there were tasks waiting for them. Thus they were given plenty of good fresh water to replenish their broken casket and more fresh fruit and provisions.

The queen promised that she would never again allow men to be tied up to the mill grindstone and she would instead have oxen pull it. New rules too, were to be passed and good relations formed with all other races. Now that their fear of water was over for the Slinkers, they would no longer mistrust people coming from the sea in ships. Everyone felt much happier.

It was time for Jack and his companions to leave. They bade their farewell to all of the Slinkers and made their way into the sea. Bobbin turned around to wave to the queen and Balena and he called, 'Don't fall into that great hole-mouth again!'

Balena waved back, with tears in her eyes, 'Come back again and see us!'

The three friends swam for the ship. On reaching it, they mended the water casket and filled it up once more with fresh water. They prepared the ship to sail, the mast was raised and with the breeze once again filling the sails, they started to move over the waves, leaving behind the Island of the Slinkers and their strange experiences there. Yet, most of all they were glad to have mended the rift between the Slinkers and the people from other islands, to have abolished slavery and to have rescued Zac. Now, it was full sail for the Island of Gumboria....

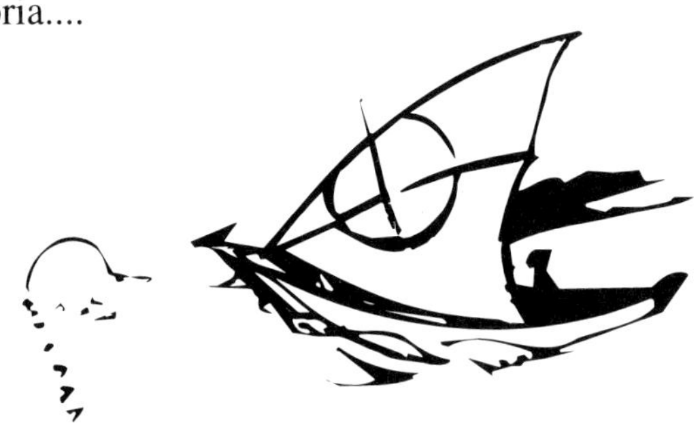

GUMBORIA, THE BEAUTIFUL ISLAND

The Island of Gumboria shone emerald in a sapphire sea. Palm and banyan trees graced her shores, while majestic mountains looked down upon the land.

Jack and Bobbin were very excited to be approaching Gumboria, but to Zac it meant something more. He was a native of Gumboria, who for over a year had been a prisoner on the Island of the Slinkers. Now he was free, and longed to be reunited with his wife and two young sons.

They were greeted with flowers and songs of welcome, for the place was home to a happy and contented people. Zac ran into the crowd to greet his wife, who had come to see the new arrivals — and what a surprise she got when she found her husband among them! Zac bid his friends farewell and returned to his home, whilst Jack and Bobbin made their way to the King's Palace.

Servants welcomed the travellers and they were ushered straight into the throne room to meet the king.

The throne room was very ornate, with elaborate carvings and paintings adorning the walls. The young men both thought it must be a very rich kingdom because of the wealth they could see displayed here. The king and queen sat on thrones amid this splendour and expressed their greetings to the visitors. Once more, as custom decreed, they were given new garments to put on (much

to the dismay of Bobbin), followed by a banquet. They were greeted with these honours in their capacity as envoys from a great king, who was a dear friend to this young king and queen.

'It was good of our dear Monarch to send two fine young men to assist us here with our dilemma.' said young King Kendal.

'Please, your majesties, enlighten us concerning the problems facing you at this time.'

The handsome young king looked despondent and then smiled.

'My father, the old king, who died a year ago, had a row with a witch who lives at the end of this island. She's wicked, and delights in causing harm, strife and commotion. Her name's Tryeena, and she can do terrible things. I've tried to make amends with her, but all in vain.

'Next week should be my coronation, but Tryeena has hidden the keys. You see, tradition states that the three keys of Gumboria should be placed into the hands of the new king... If these keys are not used, then the kingdom will become divided and chaos ensue. Anyone could then attempt to become king — even Tryeena herself! Worse still — she could win over by her witchcraft! And what a grave and terrible consequence that would have, especially upon the natives of our island.'

'What kind of keys are these?' asked Jack.

'They are three keys of gold.'

'When were the keys first noticed missing?'

'Last week. Preparations were being made for the coronation, and a guard reported that he saw Tryeena near them and thinks that she may have taken them.'

'Well, we shall just have to ask this witch outright if she's taken the keys of Gumboria.' said Jack.

So Jack and Bobbin took to the road, toward the other end of the island where the witch lived. Her home was upon a high rock with a small bridge leading to it. It was an old hovel and very eerie. Approaching the bridge, Jack called out, 'Tryeena!'

Out she came — cackling with glee. 'So! The young king has sent you here to try and bargain with me to get the keys back, he-he!'

'Surely, Tryeena, you've no grievance with young

King Kendal?'

'I do!' snapped Tryeena angrily. 'He's the son of Freedon, and I'll never forgive him for treating me so badly!'

'But King Kendal's a kind man. He'd like very much for you to forget any old prejudices and dwell in friendship now.'

'Hmh! I've no row with you, Jack, nor any malice toward that sea-boy with you. But I admit it, I've taken the keys — they're here in my home and that's where they'll stay!'

'But, Tryeena, if he doesn't get the keys, he can't be king and havoc will rule!'

'Hmm, alright. I'll give you a chance. I'll ask you three riddles, Jack, and if you're succesful in finding their meaning then I'll return one key for each riddle. But — you must find the answer by tomorrow evening, he-he! And — I want you to answer them before all the people of the island. If you fail, as you must, he-he, then at least I'll know I've not lost my powers.

'What then are these riddles you set me?' asks Jack.

'First. Bring me three red apples from the orchards of Gumboria and carry them over the bridge to my house. But, remember this — you can only carry but two of the apples with you, for the bridge will fall if you take all three, and you'll be badly hurt in the fall. Yet you must bring me the three red apples and you can only cross the bridge but once. There is a way. It can be done, but you'll have to use all your skill and knowledge to find out how to do it.

'Second. Bring to me the twins on this island that are strange — one is twenty and the other is twenty-two. If you do this, then I'll give you a second key.

'Thirdly. You are to sing me the longest song that has

ever been sung. Do these three tasks and you'll have back the keys of Gumboria for King Kendal.'

Jack and Bobbin took their leave of Tryeena and returned to report their findings to the palace. The king, astonished by Tryeena's strange conditions, gave a worried promise to Jack.

'I'll ask all my wise men to see if they can conjure up answers to these riddles.'

'Well, I have only until tomorrow evening to find the answers,' said Jack.

That evening, Jack went for a walk to be alone, and to think. As he walked by the shore, he heared laughing and splashing and looking further, saw Bobbin in the sea, and three Marlins playing with him. Bobbin tickled the huge fish under the belly, and the fish appeared to love it, for they all played with Bobbin. As the fish in the air splashed down in a sheet of spray, the third one went up into the air, while the other one jumped to the hand of Bobbin. What tremendous fun they were having! Suddenly, the clue to the first riddle dawned on Jack and he shouted excitedly to Bobbin.

'Thanks for the answer!'

Bobbin shook his head in amazement, he had no idea what Jack was thanking him for!

Walking further along the beach, Jack headed up towards the road where he met Zac, strolling happily with his wife and son in the late sunlight.

'Good evening,' said Jack, 'Is this your son?'

'Yes, it is!' said Zac, and as he spoke, another boy came running along, and Jack saw that he was a twin. 'And this is my son, too!'

Jack jumped for joy! 'Thank you, Zac, for answering the second riddle for me!'

Zac and his wife looked amazed, as they didn't recall saying anything profound, or of great importance!

Meanwhile Jack continued to walk along the road, feeling considerably happier.

He came to a field full of flowers and stopped to inhale their sweet fragrance. A large swarm of bees buzzed around him, making for the field. Every bee took a few grains of pollen and then flew back to the hive. Jack observed them for a short while, then shouted, 'I have the answer!'

His slumber that night was peaceful and deep, and refreshed his soul. As soon as he rose, he set off to find Bobbin, who always liked to sleep on the ship, and found him in the water as usual.

'Jack, why did you thank me yesterday evening?'

'Ah ha! You'll understand later today,' said Jack, as the two made their way to the palace, where all the people were getting ready to walk to the end of the island. They were all going to see if Jack could answer the witch's riddles and so get the keys of Gumboria restored to their right place. And so, at the appointed time, everyone arrived outside the hovel of Tryeena, where they waited to see the outcome of her meeting with Jack.

Tryeena came out of her house and yelled across at Jack. 'Are you ready to answer the riddles?'

'Yes,' replied Jack.

'Then come over the bridge to my house and bring me the three red apples!' she cackled. 'But remember, you can only carry two of them at a time — if you carry three, the bridge will collapse and you'll be harmed.'

'I'm ready,' said Jack and, taking the three red apples, he stood in front of the bridge. Then, to everyone's astonishment, he started to juggle the apples. He had been taught to juggle by his Uncle Tom, who had told him it might help him at a later time... The bridge was only fifty yards long and did not take Jack long to cross. Watching him, Bobbin knew what Jack had meant the evening before, for the marlins had been jumping from Bobbin's hands as if he were juggling them! Jack had simply caught onto the idea of juggling the apples, for by this method he could only have two apples in his hands at any time.

Tryeena was shocked, but she said nevertheless, 'Aw, Jack! I knew that you were not without wisdom — but you haven't won yet! Still, well done on answering your first riddle!' And she disappeared into her house and came back with the first gold key. Everyone cheered enthusiastically.

Then Tryeena said, 'He-he! Now Jack, you bring me the strange twins, where one of them is twenty and the other is twenty-two.'

Jack looked around; he could see there were several sets of twins of various ages present, so he went over to a young girl, a twin, and asked her, 'How old are you?'

'I am twenty,' she replies.

'Do you have a sister?'

'No, I have a twin brother.'

He was called over and both presented to the witch. 'Here they are,' said Jack. 'The girl is twenty and her brother twenty too.' All the folks laughed, for it was not the age that was important, but the emphasis on the word!

'Well done, once more Jack!' called Tryeena, whose harsh cackle had changed to a gentler voice. 'You are well endowed with knowledge and wisdom, I see. You'll make a good king and husband to someone one day. In fact, I wish I were not so old, or I would have cast a spell on you and kept you for myself!'

The old witch gave Jack the second key of Gumboria, and the crowd cheered again.

But then came the most difficult task of all for Jack — to sing the longest song ever invented. He had never thought of himself as a singer and felt embarrassed having to do this. Asking the king's forgiveness he started to sing this song.

'A swarm of yellow honey bees,
went flying on a summer's breeze,
And saw countless flowers beside the trees,
Hand filled with nectar up to the knees,
and one flew back to the hive.
Then another bee took another grain of pollen,
and took it back to the hive.
Then another bee took another grain of pollen,
and took it back to ther hive.
Then another bee took another grain of pollen,
and took it back to the hive.....'

Oh, but this song continued... it went on and on and on and on and on..... Jack's voice became more and more croaky and more and more harsh. His singing lacked tune and everyone became weary with this awful long, laborious song. It never changed, it went on and on and on and on... One hour passed... then two... Then five, then six hours passed... It went on for ever — or it would have — but suddenly Tryeena screamed out loud.

'Take the third key of Gumboria! Take whatever you will of me, but PLEASE — stop that dreadful noise that you call singing! I am weary of it and my head is splitting in half — eeh!'

Jack was pleased to stop singing — and all the people were relieved... Tryeena gave him the third key of Gumboria and everyone cheered.

Jack said, very hoarsely, to Tryeena, 'Why do you not come and live amongst the people of Gumboria and forget your grievance?'

Queen Trella said, 'We will be glad to give you the high tower of the palace, and it would be such a comfort to have you as our friend.'

But Tryeena wailed, 'Nobody ever loved me, and all I ever wanted was to be loved.'

Then the King spoke, 'My father did not like you because you were wicked. But now, if you wished, you could change your ways. By being kind, all the people of Gumboria would come to love you.'

Some of the children then came to her and said, 'Please! Be kind and tell us some of your wonderful stories and your adventures!'

Tryeena was touched, she told the children, 'There's nothing I would like to do more, than to tell you some of my wonderful magic stories!'

So it was then that Tryeena agreed to leave her old hovel and go to live in the luxury of the high tower of the palace. She eventually became assistant to the King and used her knowledge for the good of all.

When the King returned to the palace after the riddles were answered, he asked Jack what reward he would like. Jack asked for a ring, with which to return to the mysterious King. Kendal gave him a ring with a yellow stone.

Jack then asked King Kendal for permission to leave Gumboria, because he had urgent business elsewhere. The king ordered provisions to be put aboard the ship for

Jack and Bobbin, so that they might be ready to sail on the tide.

Bobbin was happy to be heading back out to sea, where he felt free as a bird — and most of all, he was happy to put on his old clothes once again! Jack was glad to have completed the tasks set for him, and to have the third ring that the mysterious king who sent him on these missions, had desired.

As the ship headed out to sea, and made cheerful progress back to the land where Jack's adventures had begun — all was well on board!

THE SEA-ORACLE

Returning from Gumboria, the weather was very favourable and things were going smoothly, but Jack sank into a deep and pensive mood. Bobbin seemed not to mind at first, but as the days passed, he became concerned for Jack's welfare. He plucked up courage one day and said, 'A problem shared is a problem halved!'

Jack smiled at his friend and responded. 'Yes, Bobbin, I've many things pressing on my mind and perhaps it's time for me to give you an explanation.'

Now, Jack had never really told Bobbin about his plight and had spoken only of actual events they shared together.

So Jack confided to Bobbin all of the strange story. He told him about his confrontation with Death and quest for a Land of No Death. Bobbin stood amazed while Jack related his story; he had thought that Jack was out simply to accomplish some tasks for the mysterious King. Now he had been given a deeper insight into Jack's strange motives.

Jack needed to know exactly how much time was left to him, yet there seemed to be no way of finding out. Bobbin was convinced that there was a way in which Jack could gain insight into all that was happening in the land of his home. He described his plan. In a large rock cave, there lived a great Sea-Oracle who could tell him everything he wanted to know — but, she was very dangerous. If she felt anyone asking questions was not truthful, she would kill them. In addition, she could be appeased only by a wonderful gift, something unique — something that no other person had.

'Where on earth could I find such a great gift to appease this Sea-Oracle?' asked Jack.

'There's a giant clam in the sea, very near to where we are now, who possesses a huge black pearl. The Sea-Oracle would gladly answer all your questions for such a prize,' said Bobbin. 'But, it is very difficult to get at, the giant clam is very strong, and it would take all our combined skill to retrieve it. It's closely guarded by poisonous sea-serpents. I'm lucky enough to be immune to their bite, and I've a plan we could put into action!'

So, all day, Bobbin collected strange, melon-like fruits from a coral reef. He scooped out the inner fruit, leaving only the hard skins, which he then sewed together, making them into a curious underwater suit which he presented to Jack. He told Jack how to wear this suit, so that the sea serpents would not be able to bite him. Then he rubbed Jack's hands with a foul-smelling herb, which would repel the sea serpents, for he told Jack that he must have his hands free to assist Bobbin under the waves. Bobbin explained the rest of the plan.

'The giant clam will close down on anyone who tries to enter it to gain the black pearl, so together, we shall have to put a large rock into it so that it cannot close completely. Then I shall swim inside it and, with my knife, cut at the strong muscles that give it such great strength. You, Jack, will have to be there so that we can jointly lift the pearl back up to the surface.'

Jack nodded. He was aware of the danger, although if they succeeded he might gain some vital knowledge from the Sea-Oracle.

Bobbin, armed with his sharp knife, dived into the sea and settled down next to the giant clam, from where he could see the black pearl shining with all its gem-like quality. Jack jumped into the sea too, but it took him a little while to adjust to the currents. The sea-serpents started to come round by the hundreds as soon as Jack drew near the great clam and they bit savagely at the rubbery husks of the sea fruits, whilst being repelled by the smelly, oily substance on his hands.

The giant clam stood with its cavernous mouth agape — not afraid of anything. Jack lifted a huge rock and threw it, right into the mouth of the clam. Bobbin dived quickly into the mouth as it was closing. Now, although the rock prevented it from closing right down on top of Bobbin, its strong, grinding muscles started crushing the rock as soon as it became lodged inside... Bobbin began cutting at the muscles of the clam and persisted until the clam realised that it was being destroyed from within. The clam jerked its shell open and spat out Bobbin and the black pearl.

Bobbin was shaken but unharmed and he immediately picked up the beautiful pearl and struggled with it toward the surface. Jack was being attacked by the sea-serpents, but by a stroke of luck, a huge shark came by, scattering

the serpents. It never looked closely at Jack. Bobbin and Jack hauled the large pearl up onto the ship, and fell exhausted on the deck.

When they had recovered, they made their way to the Sea-Oracle's lair. The seacave was set into the face of a tall rock. A set of steps led up to the part in which she lived and at the bottom of the rock-face was a gong, by which she might be summoned. Jack struck the gong, and immediately a thundering voice boomed out.

'What do you want with me, Jack?' She had the gift of fore-knowledge and so knew exactly who was at the door. 'What have you brought me as a present, to appease my anger for a while, so that I may tell you what you require to know?'

'I have brought you a gift of the giant black pearl from the great clam of the sea,' Jack shouted back.

Again the voice boomed out, 'I am pleased by this! You and the sea-boy may enter my home.'

Jack and Bobbin climbed up the steps that led up to her strange palace. Coloured rocks were wreathed in swirling, rainbow-hued mists, while the Sea-Oracle herself was beautiful and young-looking — Jack had expected her to be old and witch-like. She sat by a whirlpool.

'Come, sit by me, Jack. This is the pool of Wisdom and Future and if you look deeply enough into it, it will answer the questions you have in your mind that give you trouble. But the pool will answer you by sight only, you cannot speak with anything you see.'

Jack said to her, 'I understand. I should like to know how my uncles and my mother are.'

'Look deep into my pool and tell me where you wish to be.'

'I want to see my mother.' In seconds, Jack found himself in front of the porch of his mother's home, where she herself sat in a rocking chair, her eyes wide open. Jack knew his last words to her had been, 'If Death comes looking for me here, then promise me you'll never close your eyes, but look at him, straight in the face.' He knew then, that his mother was sleeping so, with her eyes open.

'I want to see my Uncle Tom next.' In seconds Jack found himself at Tom's house, although his Uncle was nowhere to be seen. 'Where could he be?' Jack asked himself... He looked toward the trees, and saw the crows stripping the bark from them... There were only a few trees left to strip and he wished Jack could speak to Tom.

'Let me now see my Uncle Dick.' In seconds Jack found himself

at Dick's home, but his uncle was nowhere to be seen. The hill of gravel and sand had dwindled to almost nothing. Jack was overcome by anxiety. He felt that time was running out. It would be virtually impossible for him to complete all the tasks that had been set for him and find the Land of No Death. 'If only I could talk to Dick for just a few moments, he could keep me up to date with all that has happened...'

'Now I would like to see my Uncle Gwillum.' In seconds Jack found himself at his uncle's home, and once again there was no sign of his uncle. Jack was now very worried.

The Sea-Oracle said, 'Now you've seen enough.'

Jack thanked the lady, although he was alarmed by what he had seen. She knew this and said, 'You still have time, Jack, before Death can catch up with you. I went with you through those waters and saw much else besides what you will have seen there; so I am able to assure you that you can still achieve the tasks you set out to do!'

Jack was much relieved by this, and as he and Bobbin returned to the ship, he could at last feel confident that he had time to complete his tasks and so find the Land of No Death. Finally after a few days sailing, they arrived back at the mysterious king's palace.

THE BEAUTIFUL PRINCESS

The butler was overjoyed at the return of Jack and Bobbin, who had now completed the three tasks that the king had set them. Jack handed the butler the ring with the yellow stone, and a banquet was given in honour of Jack and Bobbin. The butler told Jack that the king was very happy indeed, yet still could not receive them. He promised that when all their tasks had been accomplished, their reward would be great. Jack did not really want this banquet, remembering too well the visions from the sea-oracle.

Next morning, Bobbin decided to return to the ship to take care of some badly needed repairs. Jack was left to meet the butler and to hear his instructions concerning the final task for the king.

The butler now told him his final test. 'You see, Jack, the King has but one daughter — the Princess Beltarra — and by some great evil magic, she has been in a state of sleep for over a year. The king is broken-hearted. He's sent for wizards and magicians, but to no avail — none of them were able to find a cure for the strange malady that has fallen upon the princess. All who have tried to find the cause of the sleeping sickness have failed. We know that she must wake up at some-time during the night because somehow she is receiving sustenance. This must be happening at a time when everyone in the castle is asleep.

'Jack, I sincerely wish you success in your task — the King is convinced that you are his last hope. His joy will be great when you achieve this task, for not only will he then be able to receive you formally — he will also greet you as a son!'

Jack found the butler's story amazing. The butler led him to the princess's room, showing him different parts of the castle as they went, including the magnificent throne room, where Jack would be received and rewarded if he was able to complete the final task. Eventually, Jack was escorted into a beautiful, golden room where elaborate and ornate tapestries and priceless paintings adorned the walls. Near a balcony, hung with satin and silk, was the princess's bed. Jack was only allowed to enter this room as he was accompanied by the butler. The King's guards were stationed outside the door so that no wizard or sorcerer could steal away the beautiful princess.

As Jack looked around the room he saw a little white and black dog, with a black-patch around his eye. The dog seemed to be happy to see Jack and barked in friendship and came right up to him. There was also a beautiful blue bird perched outside its cage, that occasionally flew around the room. The butler told Jack that these were the princess's devoted pets.

Jack looked upon the sleeping face of Princess Beltarra, and he fell deeply in love with her. 'She's the

most beautiful creature I've ever seen! I can't understand why anyone could wish to harm her!'

'I'm afraid, Jack, that there are many evil wizards in the world today, and it was a particularly evil one that came to ask the hand of the princess. When she refused and her father would not give her to him — this was the result.'

'That's terrible!' exclaimed Jack. 'Still, it makes me all the more determined to accomplish this task! I promise I'll cherish this dear to my heart and keep it more sacred than my own life. I'll not rest until I've completed all that's required of me.'

'Splendid!' said the butler. 'Tonight, then, you may stay here alone with the princess, to see if you can find out what happens to her, or where she goes to find food.'

Jack returned to his room, to save his energy for the task ahead and to be ready so as not to fall asleep at night like the rest of the castle folk.

Later that evening, he returned to the princess's room, where the guards let him in. As he went over to sit on a chair near her bed, the little dog came to him and jumped up on his lap. The bird rested on top of the cage. The evening was warm and they were all glad of the cool breeze coming in through the balcony windows. Jack sat still and waited for something to happen.

All of a sudden, the little dog started to get excited and Jack was aware something was about to happen. He quickly hid behind the princess's bed, from where he could observe all that was taking place within the bedroom. Firstly, the dog's activities were strange: it seemed to leap about the room yelping, as if it were trying to frighten off someone, or something. Jack prepared himself to discover at last how it was that the princess received her daily nourishment. Secondly he noticed that the little blue bird had started flying excitedly round the room, and that from its tail feathers there appeared to be a fine blue dust flying out everywhere. Something was quite definitely happening... Jack opened his eyes wide to see what would unfold. He peered into the room, keeping a special watch on Princess Beltarra. He looked round towards the guards at the door, but they were all asleep! He was about to shout at them for being asleep — when he realised — it was morning...!

He too, had fallen victim to the strange sleep that attacked the people of the castle every night. A whole evening had passed and Jack could give no account of it... What had actually taken place? Had the princess gone anywhere? These questions remained unanswered, leaving Jack in the morning, full of sad thoughts despite having been so confident the evening before. He too had failed, and another day had dawned.

Jack was determined to see through to the end of the mystery. He refused to give up. There was still a plan that he could put into practise.

The butler met him in the morning and they both discussed what might be done.

Jack said, 'I have not given up yet, so please tell the king that I do have another idea. As far as everyone else is concerned, tell them that I have failed and that I returned to my own land this morning. I'll leave the castle today, to make it appear that I did fail and that I have left for good, but I'll return later this evening. Now, you must listen to my instructions and obey them precisely, for it is imperative that you do exactly what I ask.'

'I'll obey you to the letter, that's a promise,' said the butler.

'Good. Tonight, when I return and everything is quiet,

I want you to have a suit made for me of ivy-green — and please leave it on my bed. I shall then try to implement my plan. It is very important to keep the whole thing secret, nobody must know. Do not even tell the king of my intentions, nor even Bobbin if he asks!'

'You have my word, Jack,' says the butler.

So, Jack took his leave of the castle and made his way into a deep green forest, where he could try to work out his plan. As far as everybody else knew, Jack had returned to his own land.

Within the serenity and quietness of this forest, Jack gathered his thoughts together and recalled the knowledge he had gained from his uncles, to try to muster up a great plan for the lovely Princess Beltarra, so that she could be released from the sleeping-spell...

JACK MEETS NOGUILA

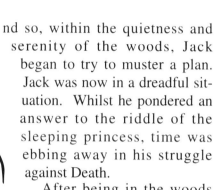

And so, within the quietness and serenity of the woods, Jack began to try to muster a plan. Jack was now in a dreadful situation. Whilst he pondered an answer to the riddle of the sleeping princess, time was ebbing away in his struggle against Death.

After being in the woods for nearly half the day, Jack decided to make a bow and arrow, because he knew that he would have to defend himself from whatever evil force attacked the castle every night. He used the branch of a young birch tree and made a long-bow. He took a few special reeds from a stream flowing through the woods to string the bow, and then he searched for a fine flint to shape into an arrowhead and feathers from a mallard duck's nest for a flight to guide it, and so made a swift arrow. Uncle Tom had taught Jack well in how to make and prepare a longbow and how to choose the correct flint for the arrow, and Jack had soon become a master archer. He fired practise shots for a while and soon adjusted the bowstrings to his precise requirements. This done, Jack decided to make tracks back to the castle.

As he came near to the edge of the woods, Jack spied a very large old man, kneeling by a pond. Jack wondered what he could be doing and observed him for a few minutes.

Jack approached and greeted the old man.

'Good day, sir.'

The old man replied, 'And a fine day to you, Jack.'

Jack was rather taken aback, 'How do you know my name?'

'I know all about you and your plight,' answered the old man, 'because I am the Wisest Wizard in Wizardom and my name is Noguila!

'I'm gathering newts presently for some of my magic spells and this pond here is especially good for them.

'You see, Jack, I'm the man who taught your uncles and they were very special pupils to me. I still keep contact with them through the eagle who carries bones in a sack, these bones are actually coded messages between us. They're all very wise indeed now and I'm very proud of them.'

'I, too, am very proud of my uncles,' said Jack.

'Come then, Jack, and I shall help you a little in your quest. You'll know by now that there's an evil spell cast upon the castle by an evil wizard, who was spurned by the princess Beltarra. He retaliated with such a wicked spell that very few magicians could revoke it. Now, although I could revoke it in seconds, I can not do so. If I were to meddle with the work of a fellow wizard I would be breaking our quite rigid code of conduct. He would be obliged to retaliate by starting an awful war of evil magic. Such a thing would be a calamity for the world and I dare not risk it. But I can tell you more details about what has happened. You see, the magician would never admit to being outsmarted by an ordinary man —

if, for instance you were able to break the spell! So, listen carefully and I will explain the whole situation. I know you're not without knowledge, so I presume you've made some preparations?'

'Yes, I have, I've asked that a suit of ivy green be made and ready waiting for me when I return to the castle. I've also made a bow and arrow, either to defend myself, or the princess.'

'Splendid, Jack! You see, nobody's ever seen the princess leave her chamber, since everyone falls into a deep sleep at night. It is during this time of sleep that she awakens.

'The first signs are when her little dog begins to get excited and bark. At the same time, the little blue bird flies all around the room and throughout the castle. On the feet of the little blue bird are drops of sleep dew and the moment the drops come into contact with anyone, they fall into a deep sleep. When everyone is sleeping the princess rises from her bed and goes to the balcony, where she turns herself into a beautiful swan and flies off into the forest, there to eat wild berries and herbs — this is how she receives nourishment. When she's eaten all she needs, she flies back to the castle, returning to her own shape and then goes back to sleep — and nobody is any the wiser.

'What you must do, Jack, is to hide in the ivy that climbs up to her balcony floor and watch as she goes away, though it's her return that is important. As she returns from her flight, you must fire your arrow straight into the heart of the swan. When she falls to the floor of the balcony, she'll sing the swan-chant. Now do you know what this swan-chant, or swan-song is?'

'Yes, my Uncle Dick once told me that of all the birds of the air or fowls of the sea, the greatest singer is the swan. Only she never sings during her life — only when she's dying will she sing what they call the swan-chant. It's the most wonderful song ever heard, but very few ever hear it.'

'Correct, Jack, your uncles have taught you well. It's imperative however, that when you shoot the swan down and she falls onto the balcony, you listen very carefully to every word she sings — for the words are her life! You must obey them. She will only sing once. This will be the crucial time for you. Therefore, use your skill as an archer to the best of your ability. Further than this I cannot help you.'

Jack thanked Noguila for his counsel and the wizard wished him luck and success in his venture. Jack then made his way back, approaching the castle silently. He tip-toed into his room, where the butler had laid on the bed the suit of ivygreen. Jack put the suit on and he returned to the castle grounds, skirting the walls until he saw the balcony of the princess's chamber, partly concealed by creepers, above him. Jack then carefully climbed up the creeping ivy that covered the wall and hid half-way up. He became completely concealed within the ivy, his suit giving him camouflage. He had a long, quiet wait. His bow and arrow were hidden deep in the ivy beneath the balcony. After a long wait, he heard the dog barking and he knew that the blue bird had started to spread her sleep dew around the castle, while all the people inside fell asleep.

Jack's body was becoming cramped, waiting in the same position, but he knew that there was no other way to save the lovely princess. The princess appeared and transformed herself into a swan that flew away to eat berries in the woods. A few hours passed and Jack became stiff and sore hiding within the ivy. Eventually he heard the flapping of wings in the distance. He prepared to fire the arrow at precisely the time and angle that the swan would land on the balcony of the room. As the swan came closer to the castle, Jack took up his stance within the ivy and manouvered his bow and arrow into the correct position. He waited for the perfect time.

Just as the swan was about to land on the balcony, Jack spoke,

'Arrow, arrow, from me part, straight into the swan's heart.'

And he let it fly.

The arrow flew straight and true to pierce the heart of the swan. The swan floundered and fell onto the floor of the balcony. As her life ebbed away she sang her swan-chant and Jack listened attentively.

He heard a wonderful voice singing these words:

'My body is made of silver, my wings are made of gold.
Take a feather from my back and into the wound you fold.'

Jack, spellbound for a few seconds by the beauty of her song quickly climbed on to the balcony. There he saw the beautiful swan lay dying, the arrow straight into her heart. He took a feather from her back and he folded it into the deep wound. Immediately, the swan's form altered into her former human body. The wound was no longer in her heart, but on her leg, so Jack pulled her quickly inside the chamber and attended to it. He bound the wound with a piece of linen from her bed. As he lifted her onto the bed she awoke. The spell had at last been broken. The whole castle wakened and there was a great hustle and bustle.

The butler came in rejoicing! 'At last!' he shouted, 'At

last! My master, the King can now receive you. He is filled with joy!'

The butler led Jack to the throne room where, on the throne, sat the king with his beautiful queen beside him; they were both smiling happily towards him.

'Welcome, a thousand times, brave Jack!' said the King. 'You must be the bravest man in all the world. We were not able to receive you before, because we too were part of that wicked spell. You see, Jack, I was the little dog that tried to warn everyone when the princess was about to waken and my wife here was the little blue bird that caused everyone to sleep with the sleep dew that flew from her feet. We could not help it, for we were powerless to stop the evil. Yet how grateful we are that you pursued the tasks. From the bottom of our hearts we thank you!

'For your great valour, I shall now make you a Prince of the Realm and ask you to take my daughter the Princess Beltarra as your bride. You shall be the one to rule after me.'

Jack was very happy indeed and delighted to be offered the hand of the princess whom he loved. Yet he knew that his personal quest was not finished; he still had not found the Land of No Death. He therefore said to the king, 'Please sire, I should like very much to marry your lovely daughter the princess, but I fear we must have no wedding feast, for I need to continue my own personal quest and time is slipping fast away. I don't have many days left to accomplish my quest, indeed I must leave on the morrow with your permission. Yet, I would like to marry the princess first (if she'll have me) and, at a later date if and when I return, we shall have the finest feast that has ever been held in the land!'

The king agreed and when Jack asked the Princess

Beltarra to be his bride, she accepted gladly. That night Jack was secretly married to the princess. He explained to Beltarra that he must leave immediately, but, with Godspeed, he would return.

So, the following morning, Jack bade his princess goodbye and took his leave. The king offered Jack a fast ship, to take him back to his own land, where Jack knew he must face Death. Jack told the king that he has to return without a ship, for an evil enemy would be waiting for him and a ship would give him away.

Bobbin appeared, to bid Jack farewell and, hearing of Jack's impending doom, he pleaded, 'Let me, dear friend, take you on my back, for I shall swim you home as fast as I possibly can.'

'No, Bobbin,' said Jack, 'for you know now who my enemy is, and believe me, this endangers your life too.' Bobbin was sorry not to help Jack, who now bade everyone farewell and walked away along by the coast on his own, to work out how he might return.

He walked for about a mile, gathering thoughts to himself and wondering what to do next, when a loud voice shouted: 'Jack!'

When he looked around, he spied Noguila, the wizard.

'I can help you to return to your own land and I shall do it swiftly.'

'But I must not endanger anyone else's life,' said Jack.

'Neither you shall,' cried Noguila. The wizard took a whistle and sounded a few notes. Within seconds a very large sea-turtle came to the shore. 'Here, Jack, is your return voyage home. He will whisk you home to your own shore in no time.'

Jack thanked the wizard once more, and sat upon the back of the sea-turtle, who hurtled back at the speed of light to his very own village by the sea.

Now to face the worst enemy of all — Death! — thought Jack grimly.

JACK ENCOUNTERS DEATH

It was late afternoon when the turtle swam, with Jack aboard, back to his own land. The village looked beautiful in the sun and Jack was glad to be home again, though he knew not what fate would have in hand for him there. He wondered why he had had to go in search of a Land of No Death when in all his journeys he had found no sign of such a place.

With his feet on dry land once more, his very first concern was for the welfare of his mother. He ran to the end of the village where his mother's house stood, and where he could see his mother, sitting in a rocking chair on the porch of the house. As Jack approached her, he looked closely at the old lady, and noticed she was very still and her large blue eyes were wide open and staring — they looked dead-pan and glassy. Tenderly, two salt tears lingered on her cheeks. She was dead. Death had taken her out of spite toward Jack, and the old woman's eyes were wide open, for she had obeyed the words that Jack had spoken to her before he left — 'If Death should come looking for me, then do not close your eyes even for a second, but keep them wide open.'

Jack had not been completely without knowledge and had learnt much from his uncles, themselves pupils of the wise Noguila. As Jack gazed sadly into his mother's large gentle eyes, they fell out of her head, landing upon her lap. Quickly, picking them up and carefully putting them into a clean handkerchief in his pocket, Jack ran away and went to his Uncle Tom's house.

There, the trees were all stripped of their bark. This meant that Jack no longer had the protection of his Uncle Tom. He searched around the house, both in and out, but there was no sign of his uncle. This was very strange, because Tom seldom went out unless to go hunting or fishing, and he remembered too, when looking through the pool of the Sea-Oracle — Tom had not been at home then either.

It was to the house of Uncle Dick that Jack ran next, where he found the hill of gravel and sand as flat as a pancake, so he knew that the protection of Dick had also come to an end. Jack was afraid (though he knew he could not afford to be frightened), but he resolved to fight to the end with Death when the time came. However, there was no sign of Dick, and Jack had no idea why it was that at the time when he needed his uncles most desperately, they were not to be seen.

There was only Gwillum to go and visit now. Jack ran the whole way to his house, where he arrived panting at the door. When he pushed it open, he found, to his surprise, all of his uncles within the house. He was delighted to see them.

'I was so sure that you'd all deserted me and I was a bit afraid!'

'Welcome, Jack! You know we'd never desert you in the hour of your deepest trial,' replied Gwillum. 'We have all been working for you, and we've had to travel

far and wide to gather the things you'll need for your fight with Death, which will be very soon...

'Remember therefore — Death can be overcome, but each occasion must be different and have to it an element of surprise. You see, Jack, all of us have made our separate bargains with Death and if you win your fight, then you too must bargain with Death for your own deal. I'll

tell you what you must do, be attentive — your very life depends upon it!

'The outcome of your battle is very important to us all, Jack, as we're all the one family, and so, while you've been engaged on your quest, we've been busy getting hold of a weapon for you. Here is a sword, that's been fashioned out of the great, northern red stone. Now this stone has magical powers in as much as it can attract metals to it. You must take this weapon and use it against Death. Let me tell you about Death. He's a formidable enemy, with tremendous powers and his scythe can cut through anyone. Also, he has the power to appear from nowhere and attack, so you'll need to be constantly on your guard when you leave this house. But now I'll let Tom tell you how to fight. Go ahead Tom.'

'Jack, I've taught you the art of fighting and how to protect yourself, but with Death you'll have to be extra careful. This sword that we've devised cannot cut anything at all, but it will have the power to stick to his terrible scythe. When Death takes a swipe at you, then very quickly, you must put your sword in the way of his weapon and the moment they touch you will have to twist with all your might. The surprise of this will disturb Death for a moment, and if for a second he drops his scythe, you must catch it and throw it as far as you can into the sea. Without his scythe, Death has only the power of a weak old man and it is then that you must seize your chance. Grab the old, weak Death and carry him on your back, right into this house. But, should he get hold of the scythe again, you'll be done for! Now Dick will instruct you further.'

'Yes, Jack. Now, I'll have a circle of salt prepared for your coming into the house and you must put Death into the centre of it. There he'll be under restraint and have no power for twenty-four hours — and this is the time to make your bargain with him. I cannot tell you what to say, but just remember — you're not without knowledge! Now Gwillum will speak to you.'

'Jack, we've taught you well in the knowledge of many things, yet now comes the time to use every bit of that wisdom. With Death contained in the ring of salt for twenty-four hours, you'll have enough time to make your own bargain with him. It may be consolation to you to know that the three of us have all been in your place, so we have sympathy for what you are feeling just now. Death cannot touch us any more, because of the bargains we each made with him, using the magic skills taught us by Noguila. These skills have to be different each time, for Death is now aware of our tricks. So, while he can have no power over us any more, you don't have this special immunity yet. If you're successful and become like us, then you'll see why this is the very reason that Death has a personal vendetta against this family — it's cheated him too often! But now, Jack, you must go out and watch for Death. He'll spring upon you suddenly, so keep your wits about you. Remember that he doesn't like the sea and most likely will attack you from the land, nevertheless keep an eye on the sea also. Put into practise everything we've taught you. Go now — with our blessing!'

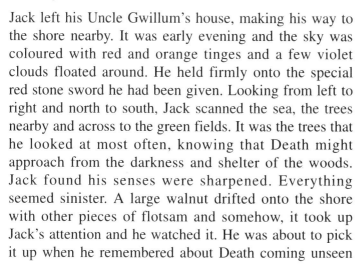

Jack left his Uncle Gwillum's house, making his way to the shore nearby. It was early evening and the sky was coloured with red and orange tinges and a few violet clouds floated around. He held firmly onto the special red stone sword he had been given. Looking from left to right and north to south, Jack scanned the sea, the trees nearby and across to the green fields. It was the trees that he looked at most often, knowing that Death might approach from the darkness and shelter of the woods. Jack found his senses were sharpened. Everything seemed sinister. A large walnut drifted onto the shore with other pieces of flotsam and somehow, it took up Jack's attention and he watched it. He was about to pick it up when he remembered about Death coming unseen upon people, so he turned quickly round again to check the trees. The moment he did so, the walnut washed up onto the shore, almost at Jack's feet, and as Jack looked round to scan the sea once more, the walnut suddenly exploded at his feet! With a flash, out came Death — his raised scythe ready to swipe into Jack — who reacted swiftly, managing to get his sword against the scythe... It connected... and Jack gave a mighty twist. The scythe fell from Death's hand into the water. Jack quickly sprang toward it, picking it up and throwing it as far as he possibly could out to sea. Death made after it to retrieve it, but not quickly enough to stop Jack from picking him up, putting him over his shoulders and carrying him into the house of his Uncle Gwillum, where all was prepared.

Jack dropped Death into the ring of salt, from where he was unable to move. How angry Death became now! Jack prepared himself to do some hard bargaining with him!

Death screamed at Jack, 'You may think you've outsmarted me, but you haven't! This family has cheated me for years and years, but now I've come for my revenge. I'll stay within this circle of salt for twenty-four hours — but then I'll return to my former strength and retrieve my scythe and you'll find you've failed. Then I shall have the power to take you away to my domain at last!'

The uncles look worried.

Then up spoke Jack. 'I am not so easily won as you may think, my dear Death, for I am not without knowledge, and my uncles have taught me well in many arts. Now let me tell you something: I am now going to leave this house and retrieve your scythe, which I shall then take in my rowing boat to The Rumbling Goiter — there I shall throw it in and watch it disappear. Now you will know as well as I that The Rumbling Goiter is the deepest whirlpool in the whole world, going right down into to the very bowels of the earth. It will therefore take you at least seven years to find it again... That should give me another seven years of protection from you, but, more importantly still — it will bring all your work to naught... For seven years, no person shall die! Why, you'll be a failure — it'll take you centuries to bring your work up to date again!'

Death looked very worried and he muttered, 'This family always find ways to cheat and make fun of me.' But then he agreed more confidently, 'All right, so you have me over a barrel and I've to grant you some small request — what'll it be?'

'First, I want your promise that you will never bother me again. Secondly, I wish to have immunity for my wife and any children that we may have. Thirdly,...'

'You ask far too much!' screamed Death.

'Och well, I'll just be off now and throw away the scythe...'

'Oh no! You mustn't do that! I'll grant you those two requests, only, but certainly nothing more.'

'But, indeed I want more! You have given me so much trouble — I had to endure many trials when you made me an exile from my own home and land. It was an anxious time, performing the many difficult and dangerous tasks, and although they've helped me to become stronger and wiser, and I've made some wonderful friends, nevertheless, when I finally married a beautiful princess you blighted my wedding night and ruined any future for me. So, I can assure you Death, you shall now pay more dearly than you can imagine, you will grant my third request.'

Jack's uncles looked on, amazed at how calmly and boldly their nephew bargained.

'Well, what is your last request?' snarled Death, pale with worry.

'I wish my mother to be returned alive — out of your hatred and malice, you took her away too soon.'

'Ha! That I cannot do, for I am limited in my powers,' yelled Death.

Gwillum now joined the conversation. 'Unfortunately, Jack, he is powerless in this, he really cannot do that request — I think you should consider yourself fortunate with what you have—'

'No!' says Jack, 'I will have all restored to me. If Death cannot do this thing then I will go now and throw away the scythe. I desire that all three of my wishes be done and I become a master like you three.' But Death, with a hoarse laugh says:

'There's only one way she could be brought back. Firstly, your mother would've had to have died with her eyes fully open and never have closed them as I took her soul away. And secondly, you would've had to have those very two loving eyes upon your person right now. Without those two preconditions nothing...'

'But I do have these things!' says Jack quietly. 'I forewarned my mother never to close her eyes if you came looking for me, because I knew that you'd take her, out of malice.'

'Let me see the loving eyes,' said Death, in disbelief. 'Hmm... Well, I've rarely seen this achieved before — yes, Jack, I'll grant you've won — your mother will be at home in her cottage when you return.'

The uncles were dumbfounded by Jack's knowledge.

Dick said, 'I think we under-estimated you, Jack!'

'Well done!' said Gwillum. 'You have graduated to being one of us — except that you've gained a throne, a princess and immunity from Death for all of your children!' And the uncles laughed!

'Yes,' grinned Jack. 'I was properly taught!'

Jack lead Death out of the circle of salt and walked with him to the sea shore, where he went into the sea and retrieved the terrible scythe. Jack knew that once Death had given his word he would stand by it. Death then confessed to Jack.

'Perhaps I am angry at being beaten once again by your family, Jack. But, I must admit, you've been a worthy opponent and deserve all you asked of me. Believe me then when I say that I no longer have any ill-feeling toward you. If the scythe was lost for seven years, I'd never have caught up with my proper work. And it was in malice toward you that I took your mother away. So, let's shake hands and remember malice no more.'

Jack agreed, they shook hands and went their separate ways.

What a relief for Jack and his uncles, who came to congratulate him on his success. Jack hurried off to look for his mother whom he found none the worse for her ordeal — indeed, she remembered nothing of being with Death. So, as all the adventures were recounted to her and the three uncles, she more than any marvelled at the stories.

All Jack's friends were delighted to see Jack back in the village, and even the little magpie (the one who first brought Jack the bad news of Death) sang Jack a special, happy song.

Now Jack arranged for a large ship to take all his family back to the land where the Princess Beltarra lived and where a proper wedding could now take place. Only this time, Jack would be arriving as a prince endowed with wealth and prosperity. All his friends would be invited.

Everyone gathered and climbed aboard the ship, to sail to the land where first Jack landed in a sack of bones carried on the wings of the diamond Eagle.

THE MARRIAGE FEAST

Princess Beltarra looked over her father's high castle wall towards the sea.

She had kept up this ritual from the day that her husband Jack, had left. There was hope in her heart and she longed for the moment of his return. As she scanned the horizons as usual this morning, she thought she could see a large ship out on the main, and as she kept up her vigil the sails soon could be seen. The wind was carrying this ship at full sail straight toward her, and as it approached she saw that it was filled with many people. Searching the faces, she found her beloved one and she let out a sharp scream. The king and guards came running, thinking something had frightened the princess, and indeed her face was wet with tears.

The King cried, 'What's happened to frighten you, my dear?'

'It's Jack! He's bringing that ship to land — he's come back!'

Everyone was full of excitement, for now at last, the marriage feast could begin. The princess quickly adorned herself in the finest of silks to look her best for her husband! The whole country rejoiced at their reunion with every home throughout the land celebrating the event.

The castle was festooned with garlands and the cooks prepared the most splendid banquet ever held in the land. Musicians were brought from far and near to perform for the happy couple, and magicians were invited to show their skills as well. Nothing was spared for the feast.

There were some surprises in store. The king had known of Jack's return, because old Noguila, the Wisest Wizard in Wizardom, had told him when this would be. And so, to Jack's surprise, all of the young rulers from the islands of Madaras, Horgan, Gumboria and even the Slinker Queen and her daughter were present. Noguila especially invited them because Jack had touched all their lives for the better. Apart from these and all the other dignitaries, all Jack's own friends and relatives were present at this celebration.

With everyone seated at the many tables, the old King gave his speech to honour Jack.

'Jack here, is the worthiest person that I have ever encountered. He has all the qualities needed to make a good king and ruler, and he shall rule after me. I, along with many of my wise councillors, will assist in preparing him for this. Will you all therefore join me in wishing Jack a long and happy life with my dearest daughter, Beltarra!'

(Each of Jack's uncles winked at each other and looked toward Noguila, for they all knew that since Jack had beaten Death, a long life was inevitable for Jack and his loved ones!)

The King asked Jack to bestow any honour or title on anyone whom he felt deserved it. Jack turned to Bobbin, who was sitting near him. 'I would like to grant Bobbin

the first request.'

'Well, there are two requests, Jack, that I should really like granted,' replied Bobbin. 'I should very much like to own the little ship we used to search the islands in, so that I may go in search of my own true identity...'

'Indeed, you shall have that ship, Bobbin.'

'And secondly, I wonder if I might request that the maiden Maera from the island of Mardaras be summoned to be Lady-in-Waiting to your bride, if it would please your princess, for she's the nearest person to me that I know of. And although we are of different beginnings, somehow we both have an affinity with the sea.'

Jack answered, 'If the King of Mardaras allows this then most certainly it will be granted.'

The King of Mardaras nodded his consent. Bobbin was delighted. 'Thank you both very much. It will be good to have a friend who feels as much at home in the sea as on land, and know too that she will be here each time I return — for I must now find out more about myself and the maiden Maera.'

Each of the young rulers paid tribute to Jack, describing to the old king how much he had taught them.

The Wizard of Horgan stood up and said:

'Yes, Jack is the bravest and wisest man I know. He's an obedient and tireless worker — I owe to him my reinstatement as advisor to the king once more, and he's fully deserved all he has now gained.'

Noguila, Wisest Wizard of all, gave a short speech in honour of Jack:

'Jack's done everything he's been asked, not running in the face of the enemy, but going forward always. He has been aware of the feelings of others and listens and acts upon his own intelligence, turning knowledge to wisdom by applying good sense and working to the best of his advantage. Truly, he will make a wise ruler and many shall come to him for this in the future.'

Jack replied: 'I, now, am grateful to each of my uncles, who taught me many great things and by whose example I now am who I am. My mother has been an inspiration to my life and brought me up to know the blessings of hard work. I hope she'll stay here at the castle with us and now rest from her labours to enjoy all that we can offer her.'

There were plenty of other speeches after that and music, dancing and entertainment which lasted for well over three days. Everyone in the land was allowed a holiday and was given a gift.

At last Jack had fulfilled his quest and found that great things are achieved by simple honesty and labour. Now that he could relax from the prospect of Death on his heels, he had indeed found the true Land of No Death. He and his princess would live happily forever and bring up a fine family of children who were in no danger from Death. His life now held deep meaning and satisfaction.

As for Bobbin, he was about to embark on a new task to find his true identity and was to have many more experiences of the sea and many, many more adventures.

THE SEA-QUEST

King Jack gave his friend Bobbin, the sea-boy, the highest honour in the land for his brave services. Bobbin was declared a freeman of the land, the only person in the kingdom to have such special privileges. Bobbin no longer had to stand in great ceremony before the king and queen, or wear costly apparel and robes of state. For this boy hated dressing-up. Bobbin's great pleasure was to spend all day in the same clothes — those that he used for swimming in the sea.

During his stay in King Jack's realm, (known now as the Land of no Death) Bobbin spent most of his time making ready his ship. There were many repairs to attend to, for she needed a complete overhaul to make her truly sea-worthy. Bobbin had painted and tarred the wood and replaced all old and water-logged wooden planks with fresh, strong timbers. Provisions were put in the hold and all the old water barrels were replaced with new air-tight ones, whilst there were plenty of extra supplies stored on board for times of emergency.

For somehow it seemed Bobbin was unable to settle down anywhere. A strange melancholy often seemed to overpower him and make him sad. Something vital was missing in his life and he did not really know what it was. When he sat upon the high cliffs overlooking the sea he could hear the wailing cries of the whales and the dolphins. This would make him dive from the rocks into the sea so that he could be nearer that feeling of belonging, for always it seemed imperative that he should find his origins, or otherwise that feeling of home sickness would kill him. The boy struggled deeply within his soul. Only the sea knew his answer.

The maiden Maera occasionally visited him, but at times she too wore that same woe begone look that Bobbin had. Queen Beltarra was kind to Maera, now her lady-in-waiting, and permitted her to go out to swim whenever she desired, which made life tolerable for her. Bobbin's spirit was more restless. The answer for him seemed to lie in the sea, and Bobbin was determined to find the solution of his origins.

The lady who had brought him up had been kind to Bobbin. She had other children to look after, and Bobbin had known from an early age that he was not really one of her offspring. Since he was seven years old he had lived on his own and only occasionally now would he visit his earth-mother. She was always glad to see him and he, in turn, always provided her with a pearl or two so that she and her family would never go hungry. Sometimes he brought her special delicacies from the sea.

The time had now come for Bobbin to ask her how she

had found him. Bobbin went to see her and asked, 'When and where did you find me, Mother? I must now discover my true identity.'

'Bobbin, I never found you... It was an old fisherman with his small net, fishing among a shoal of tuna fish, pulling up his net, who spotted a silver box. He thought that it might be a genie or a wailing sea-demon within

the box. It was too dangerous to open it there on the sea, so he waited until he reached land. He rowed his boat and catch back to the shore where he opened up the silver box. Inside there was a green seaweed shawl, and when he opened that, there, inside was a little boy! This tiny child had a strange wave of hair that seemed to move and shimmer in the sun... Being an old man he didn't know how to take care of one so young, so he brought you to me... When I took the baby out I found a little medallion tied round his toes. It was made of silver and jade. I wanted to sell it to buy food for my children but I couldn't. You see, Bobbin, I've kept this medallion safe ever since, because I knew that one day you would ask me about your beginnings.'

She handed Bobbin the medallion and there, upon its surface, was a strange form of writing and inscriptions. A salt tear fell from Bobbin's eyes... At last, proof that showed him that he was not a natural land dweller!

'What about the silver box?'

'The old man took the silver box and sold it in another land. The depths of his poverty told him that such a box would fetch a fine price in another land. In my own hardship, whilst I was frequently very tempted to sell the medallion, I did not. It is yours. You have enriched my life and given me so many gifts that I feel you to be my own son. Yet you're a very independant lad, Bobbin. Let me now give you my blessing before you go on this quest to find your true identity. And always know that I will forever love you.'

His foster-mother then laid her hands on his head and gave him her blessing. Bobbin, bidding his mother farewell, returned to his ship, where all was now set for his next voyage.

Maera came to the ship to bid him God-speed on his new adventure and so did King Jack and Queen Beltarra...

Bobbin, alone at last on his ship, set his sails high to catch the southerly winds, and sailed away with the setting sun shining brightly in the west.

Where would he go? What direction should he follow? Would he let his wild sea-instincts take over, or should he follow some true course? He was now sailing towards the south, and in his mind Bobbin had a reason for this. He had decided to go and visit the strange Sea-Oracle once more. The Sea-Oracle held the power and knowledge to reveal his origins. Bobbin felt certain that she would be able to set him in the right direction to begin his quest.

Eventually, after three days of sailing and favourable winds, Bobbin reached the rocky shore where the Sea-Oracle dwelt. Knocking upon the great gong to summon her, he waited for her response.

'What present have you brought me sea-boy?'

Bobbin had come prepared.

'Your Majesty of the sea, I bring the mirror, comb and brush of an earthly queen, so that you may brush your long beautiful hair.'

'Then you are welcome sea-boy!'

Bobbin was admitted into her huge cavernous domain.

'I see by my all-seeing eye that your friend Jack has been successful in his quests and that he has beaten Death! So, what do you want to know from me?'

'Yes, Jack has done all the things he set out to accomplish. Now, I have a need to know of my own origins.'

'I know who you are — but even I am not permitted to tell you everything at this time. I can however set you well upon your travels.'

'I would be most grateful if you could set me in the right direction,' replied Bobbin.

'Have you ever heard of the Green Man of Positive-thinking, Bobbin?'

'Yes, at least I've heard of the legend. Does he really exist?'

'Indeed he does, but he is very dangerous. Do you know where he dwells?'

'No, great Oracle, I don't know where he dwells.'

'He dwells upon an island called the Patterns of Vexors. It is no ordinary island. It is a living organism that grows and feeds on foolish people. Sometimes it vanishes into the sea, whereas quite suddenly it will reappear and be just like a green island again. The Green Man of Positive-thinking asks any stranger who ventures upon the land believing that it is an island, three questions. If you do not answer positively — then you will become his prize possession. If you are captured he will keep you to fatten up in preparation for the feast of Neptune — you will be going there at the most dangerous time — you could end up as his celebration dinner!'

'I've no intention of letting that happen!' said Bobbin.

'Let me help you then, Bobbin.' The Sea-Oracle took out three sea-sweets. 'Before answering the Green Man, firstly listen carefully to his question and then suck one of my sea-sweets. Their vapours are the same vapours that give me my great powers of knowledge. These sweets will open your mind to positive-thinking.'

Bobbin took the sweets and thanked the Sea-Oracle for her kindness. A new spirit of adventure filled him. He could go out in the knowledge that he was closer to his beginnings than he had ever been before.

Returning to his ship he breathed in the sea air, filling his lungs with the sea breeze to allow his instincts to take him to the Patterns of Vexors. The sea air in his nostrils and lungs stimulated the waves on his head as he set sail in a south-westerly direction.

PATTERNS OF VEXORS

By keeping to a south-westerly sailing route, Bobbin thought that he should come to somewhere in the vicinity of the Patterns of Vexors. His instinct usually kept him on a direct course, yet despite the scent of land he could see no sign of any island.

He sat for hours on the crow's nest, looking through his spy-glass. He could not fathom why he could smell the land so strongly.

It was now the third day of pleasant winds and still no land could be seen. As far as the eye could reach in every direction there was nothing. While steering a straight course and keeping a vigilant watch the smell of land became suddenly overpowering. This was too much for Bobbin. Nothing in front or to either side, he turned around and — behold — there was a small green island that just seemed to have appeared out of the sea!

Hundreds of seagulls emerged from the water and Bobbin knew that this was truly the Patterns of Vexors.

The birds must have found cover in its underground caves so that they might fly out whenever it resurfaced again. Bobbin knew that now at last he had found the large living organism.

The island itself looked moist and verdant, with all kinds of luscious vegetation growing there. Not only that, there were various beautiful kinds of seaweed growing upon its rocks. Any passer-by might think it was just a green island, however underneath this green covering there lay a most sinister creature. Bobbin remembered the Sea-Oracle's words about the old Green Man of Positive-thinking.

Bobbin anchored his ship close by the Patterns of Vexors and swam the short distance to reach the island. It was indeed beautiful, and sweet and salty smells filled

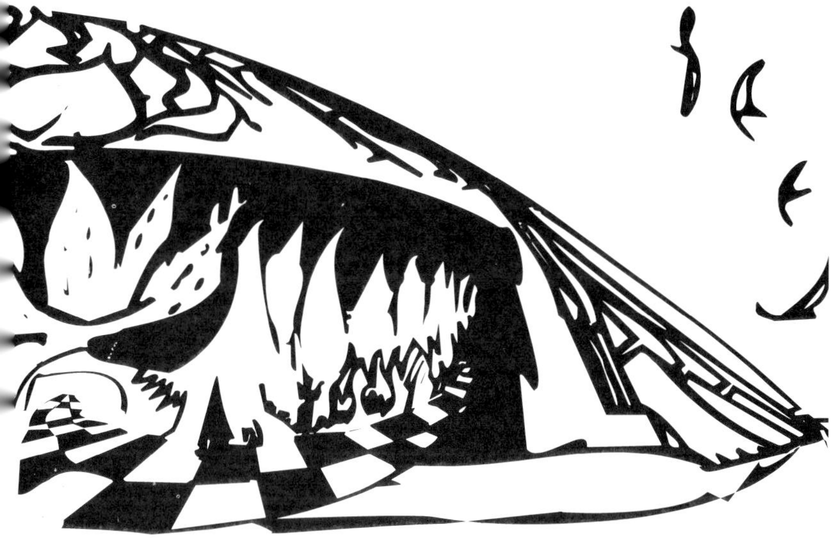

the air. Away to the far side of the island he could see an old man dressed in green clothes who was gathering coloured pebbles.

Approaching the old man with great caution Bobbin kept his wits sharp. And when the Green man caught sight of Bobbin he fairly skipped about like a mad thing — why! — he seemed overjoyed that a stranger should come to visit him on the green island. Bobbin walked over and shook his hand, but it was like shaking a dead fish. There was a slimy undercurrent from it, and the hair on Bobbin's head instinctively began to rustle and shimmer. Bobbin knew well that all was not what it appeared to be, and if the old man seemed to be friendly... well, he did have an ulterior motive in his heart!

'Dear friend, wonderful sea-boy! Come and have dinner with me! I lack company and it is a great pleasure for me, a lonely, harmless old man, to receive someone like you!'

'Thank you for your hospitality,' Bobbin replied clearly, for he was now honing-up his wits, knowing that once he was in the living organism's domain then the old Green man might become sinister and show his true colours.

The old man led him up to a small hilltop, where a passageway led below the earth. Once underground, bright lights beamed from the walls and a distinct sulphuric smell was prevalent. Bobbin followed the man until they reached a large, bright room, where a table was set with many different kinds of vegetables and seafoods upon it. The spacious room was decorated with pictures and glittering chandeliers, and candles.

'Come, sit down — dear sea-boy, and my poor servant will give you your fill, and — whatever be your pleasure — he can provide for you!'

Hunger was gnawing at Bobbin's stomach and he was looking forward to a nice meal, but never for a moment did he allow his will and concentration to slip, because too much depended upon his straight and positive thinking.

A strange-looking creature came into the room carrying a silver platter with many sea-delicasies. What a bizarre creature this was! It stood about three feet high and was fat and podgy. Its head was fat too, with very large, pale blue eyes. Overall, it looked like a dark-blue, fat jelly with plump, short little legs and arms. Instead of ordinary hair he had yellow tentacles, that were stringlike and slightly paler blue than the rest of his body, whilst around his middle he wore a short grass skirt. Perhaps the most peculiar part of all was the black leathery dots that were all over his body. Whatever he was, he was the funniest looking creature that Bobbin had ever seen — and he had seen many a strange sight during his many adventures and travels!

As Bobbin looked curiously at the creature he felt a sadness for it as well. Probably this too was a creature caught in the snare of the Patterns of Vexors, who was now a servant to the old Green Man of Positive-thinking.

'Please, what are you?' Bobbin asked politely.

The creature wobbled and laughed, and then in a booming voice replied, 'Sir, I am a bamfoon.'

'A bamfoon? I've never heard of such a thing!'

'Well, we live on an island in the middle of the sea, about two hundred miles from here. One day, whilst I was in my boat, a sudden hurricane came and carried me away for many miles until I landed up in the middle of this strange sea. There was not a sight of land, until after a couple of days, this island just appeared. I thought I was saved, for on landing here I was greeted by the Green Man, who gave me a nice meal and made me feel quite at home. Then, after the meal, he asked me three questions. I failed to answer them correctly, so he made me his servant. I've been up and under this island for over nine months—'

The old man interrupted, 'Stupid bamfoon, will you stop speaking nonsense and attend to your duties!'

The bamfoon left immediately. Bobbin asked, 'Is it true you'll not let the bamfoon off the island and that you keep him here as your servant and prisoner?'

'Yes, I do! And you too will end up like him if you do not answer the questions correctly.'

'I've no desire to live here on the Patterns of Vexors, nor do I fancy being your servant for long,' snorted

Bobbin.

'Well, if you do not get the answers correct then you will only be my slave for a few days!'

'You mean you'll let me off?'

'Certainly not. I intend to have you for my Feast of Neptune. You see, it is only a few days away and once I fatten you up you will make a wonderful meal! That was what I was keeping the bamfoon for — he was going to be my meal for the celebration — but now I have a far sweeter specimen!'

'If I can answer your questions then what will happen to me?'

The old Green Man replied, 'I am bound by honour and truth to let you go unharmed, and I am also oath-bound to help you with your quest.'

'Then let us delay the agony no longer — ask me the questions,' said Bobbin.

The old man took him to a large pool within his domain, which Bobbin could see was a tidal pool fed by the sea. The old man pointed to the pool, which was at the half-water mark.

'You see before you a pool of sea-water. It is at the half-water mark. Tell me truly — is it half-full of water or is it half-empty?'

Bobbin looked surprised at the question. The answers seemed exactly the same to Bobbin. Putting a small sea-sweet into his mouth he hesitated a moment before giving the answer. Strong vapours were emitted from the sweet and the power of the Sea-Oracle fell upon him. He could see clearly and his mind was alert to positive thinking. 'Your pool is half full. When it fills it will be full. If it were half empty then when it ran out it would be empty. To be full is positive but to be empty is negative.'

'Well done on your answer, for it is correct. But secondly — look into my pool where you can see my zebra fish. Are they black with white stripes or white with black stripes?'

Popping another sea-sweet into his mouth, Bobbin again let the vapours filter through his nostrils, clearing his mind and leaving it open to positive thoughts. Pausing briefly, Bobbin allowed his mind to unfold, 'They are neither black with white stripes, nor are they white with black stripes but they are equally divided. There are five white stripes and five black stripes. One colour does not have precedence over the other.'

'Well done again,' cried the old Green Man.

Finally the old man asked, 'Which is the largest of the sea-creatures? Is it the white whale or the blue whale?'

This was an unusual question and Bobbin knew that there was more to it than any of the others.

He let the vapours of his last sweet fill his being once more and the great wisdom of the Sea-Oracle fell upon him so that he could understand the question fully.

'You asked me, old man, to tell you which is the largest of the sea-creatures and then you complicated the question by putting on another part which is not relevant to the first part. You added on the second part to confuse me!

'For, you see, it is nothing to do with the whales. What you really want to be told is who is the largest of the sea-creatures? We are now both on the largest of the sea-creatures. For it is surely the Patterns of Vexors that is the largest of all the sea-creatures. It is as big as an island, but it is a living thing.'

'Well, well. Never before have I found anyone with so much knowledge of things of the sea,' cried the old man. 'You have truly earned your freedom and I am bound now by my own laws to give you help on your travels. Though I shall be sorry that you will not be gracing my plate for the Feast of Neptune. It will have to be the bamfoon after all.'

Bobbin asked then, 'Old man, where do you think my origins began? I have this medallion with some inscriptions upon it. Could you translate it for me?'

'My knowledge lies not in translation, but perhaps I can surmise where you are from. I believe you are one of the natural sons of Neptune himself, yet the only way you can find that out for sure is to sail to the Isle of Neptunia. It is two days sailing, favourable winds permitting, and you need to travel eastward toward the rising sun.'

Bobbin was thrilled! Was he truly a son of the King of the Sea — of Neptune himself? 'I'll leave as soon as possible,' he said to the old Green Man. Bamfoon then appears on the scene looking helpless and sad.

'Old man, you're not really going to eat the bamfoon for the Feast of Neptune are you?'

'Yes. Unless of course you can tempt me with something of a more flavourable nature?'

'Perhaps I do have something better. Would you give me a couple of hours to see what I can find for for you?'

'Alright, but return swiftly, for I will soon have to submerge once again to live under the sea.'

Bobbin ran out of the underground room and onto to the shore of the island, where he whistled across the sea. In a few minutes a large marlin came to the island. Bobbin jumped on the back of the huge fish and holding on to the large dorsal fin whistled again. The marlin went along the waves like lightning, not stopping until it came to a deep underwater coral reef, where Bobbin swam down beneath the waves until he came to a narrow crevice in the reef. Sliding his way through, this led him into a secluded sea-orchard where delicious red clam fruits and blue gosplins flourished. He gathered a few, tied the fruit to his side, and then clambered back through the opening to where the giant marlin was waiting to take him back to the Patterns of Vexors.

On arriving back he felt the great vibration of the island, which already looked as if it was preparing to submerge. Bobbin ran below to the old Green Man and showed him the delicious fruits. The old man gave the bamfoon to Bobbin in fair exchange for the wonderful fruits which he knew would taste far better.

Bobbin and the bamfoon hastily dived into the sea. The gulls had all retreated back inside the island. With a fierce crash the Patterns of Vexor sank back into the sea, causing a huge swell. The waves from the sinking island flung both Bobbin and the bamfoon for nearly a quarter of a mile. Once the waters had settled they swam easily towards the ship. Bobbin was a superb swimmer, but the bamfoon just floated about. He had the strangest style of swimming, rather like a giant jelly-fish.

They both swam along, until Bobbin spied a large shark coming towards them. 'Hurry! We must get back before the shark gets us!'

Bobbin swam furiously, but the bamfoon could not make progress. As soon as Bobbin reached the safety of the ship, he looked about him for the harpoon so that he

could rescue the bamfoon, but even as he looked he could see the shark making directly for the bamfoon. Just as the shark closed in to attack, Bobbin noticed an underwater explosion taking place. He saw a large yellow stain, followed seconds later by a purple shock wave. The shark reeled about in the water whilst the bamfoon managed to get away to safety and reach the boat. Bobbin helped his new found friend aboard.

'A very fortunate explosion for you, bamfoon, but it certainly knocked that shark about! I'm going to Neptunia, but I'll set you free on your own land sometime along the way. You see, it's very important for me to find my roots and my true identity.'

The bamfoon was very grateful to Bobbin for saving him from being a dinner for the old Green Man on the Patterns of Vexors. Bamfoon asked that Bobbin allow him to accompany him, at least on the next stages of his quest.

'Then let's make sail for the Isle of Neptunia and see what new adventures greet us there!'

Bobbin set his sails and travelled in an easterly direction, hoping that in two days time they would be at the Isle of Neptunia. Fair trade winds seemed on their side and so the ship sailed out to meet a horizon facing the rising sun.

TWINS OF NEPTUNIA

Twin towering peaks, almost identical, gave to the Island of Neptunia an unmistakable character. Slight mists drifted around the soaring heights and scented breezes wafted abroad.

Both Bobbin and bamfoon had mixed feelings.

'I wonder what fate lies for us in there.' said Bobbin.

'Perhaps some clues to your origins,' replied Bamfoon.

There was a small secluded harbour, where Bobbin decided to berth his ship. It was only a few minutes walk from there into the heart of the city of Neptunia. The inhabitants gave them strange looks, and Bobbin felt a complete stranger there. Surely, if he was akin to the Neptunians then he should feel some affinity with the place? But everything felt alien to him. The people here were a very dark, swarthy race, and all of them were tall. Bobbin on the other hand was fair-complexioned. Cautiously, the pair made their way up to the large building that they took to be the royal residence. They were greeted by soldierly-looking guards.

'Cast down your weapons and you may be admitted into the Princes' hall.'

'We have no weapons, as we come in peace. There is no anger or malice in us. Only a desire to find more knowledge,' said Bobbin.

Bamfoon only chuckled and everybody thought that he must be indeed a very strange creature.

Eventually they were admitted into the royal hall, where there stood three thrones. One large throne was positioned in the middle and two smaller ones stood on either side. On the small thrones sat two small, young, swarthy men. Although they looked like humans, down the sides of their necks they both had gills. All the people had these strange neck gills which gave them a very fishy, reptilian look. These young princes were identical twins. And, just like the twin peaks, the young princes could not be told one from the other. One of them spoke, stating, 'I am Prince Cloudio and my brother is Prince Mistyo. We are the true sons of the great King Neptune, Lord of the Seven Seas.'

Then the other one spoke, 'Our father usually rules and this large throne is his, but during his absence we attend to all the government of the kingdom. Neptune has so many duties to see to, that very often he must be absent from the land. We share the kingdom equally during his absence. There is no fighting over who is the senior of us because our father has devised a cunning means to satisfy us both.'

Cloudio piped up again, 'You see, I rule during the time when the clouds and rain come to the land and my brother Mistyo rules during the times of mist and fog. We are both happy with this arrangement. At all other

times we make decisions together because that is the time when father reigns. Even in his absence he is king, but he does give us the opportunity to both serve as kings.'

Bobbin grasped the opportunity to greet the princes formally. 'I am pleased to meet you both. I come here on a special quest to find my own origins. The old Green Man of Positive-thinking told me that he thought that the key to my origins may be here and that I could also be a son of Neptune.'

The young princes looked at each other thoughtfully.

'Obviously you're not one of our race, and you are definitely no brother of ours,' said Mistyo.

Cloudio shook his head and said, 'Sorry, dear friend, you are not a Neptunian. If you were one of us you would have gills on your neck. I'm afraid you belong to another race of sea-people.'

Bamfoon just gave a sort of chuckle and said, 'Well, Bobbin, never mind, we all belong to somebody or something.' The two princes made a kind of grin, but their mouths were permanently shaped in a downward fish-like manner.

Mistyo said, 'You must stay to have a nice meal with us,' and he snapped his webbed fingers. Then many servants appeared with large bowls of live fish. Neither Bobbin nor bamfoon could eat live or raw fish, they preferred their fish cooked.

Both Mistyo and Cloudio opened their mouths very wide revealing a row of razor-sharp teeth like that of a shark and they devoured many of these live fish.

'Do you not like our food?' cried Cloudio.

'Begging your pardon, sire, but neither my friend nor I can eat raw or live fish.'

Mistyo laughed and cried out aloud, 'Then you are

definitely not one of our kind, as we are very partial to live fish.'

'What is that medallion you have around your neck?' asked Cloudio.

'This is the only clue and evidence of my origins.'

'Let me see it,' said Cloudio. 'Perhaps I can decipher the message.'

The young prince could make neither head nor tail of it, and he handed it over to his twin brother who was as baffled as he by the inscription.

Mistyo then cried out, 'The wizard of Horgan can read this language. He is a fluent scholar in all marine languages. Do you know of the Wizard of Horgan?'

'Yes. He is a close friend of mine,' replied Bobbin.

'Then I would take your medallion to him and have him translate it for you,' said Cloudio.

Some cooked food and fruit was brought in and served to the guests. It was delicious.

All of a sudden Mistyo said, 'I remember where I have seen that medallion writing before. It is part of father's treasure trove, down in the underwater cave. There's an amulet, I think, on top of the third chest. It's made of silver and jade and has those same inscriptions on it.'

Bobbin's hair shimmered with excitement. 'Then there was need for me to come to this land after all! A vital clue to my beginnings is to be found here.'

Cloudio said, 'Well, if you can retrieve it from the underwater treasure house, then you may have the amulet, because my father is not a thief. Neither are we.'

'That's very kind of you, young princes!' replied Bobbin excitedly.

Mistyo cautioned Bobbin not to be over excited; the treasure was not easy to get access to, because the treasure-house was underwater and guarded by an evil denison. This beast was a Gleek and immensely powerful, it would eat Bobbin without hesitation.

Mistyo continued, 'The treasure trove is like a jail with large bars, wide enough for you to swim through but not wide enough for the Gleek to enter. If you can get to it and back in safety, then by all means the amulet is yours.'

'Then I'll wait no longer,' cried Bobbin.

'I will come with you to help; in case you run into trouble,' said bamfoon.

'Personally, I think you'll be more of a hindrance to me. I would only worry about you as you aren't a good swimmer underwater — you wobble about too much.'

Bobbin caught a hurt look in the big blue eyes of bamfoon and he immediately rectified his statement. 'But what would I do if you weren't there to help me and I got caught by the Gleek?'

The big smile returned to the face of bamfoon and he chuckled a bit more.

They were led to the steps of the underwater treasure-house where the water was very deep and cold. Bobbin dived in smartly, while the bamfoon clumsily wobbled over the side, swimming in jerky movements. With smart strokes Bobbin found the prison-like treasure trove and looked about for the Gleek. The Gleek was nowhere to be seen. Bobbin quickly swam over the many chests and indeed found the special amulet. It was the same as his medallion; seemingly all part of the same piece. Surely this must be the reason why they had come to Neptunia. He was very pleased. With the amulet picked up, Bobbin darted towards the bars of the trove. Quickly, he was through the bars and felt he had made it safely, though bamfoon was still at the other side of the treasure house.

Bobbin held up the amulet and showed bamfoon it was safe.

Suddenly, a huge boney hand with sharp claws clutched his arm. A monstrous creature with a huge head and cavernous jaws had appeared from nowhere. It was a Gleek. Bobbin could feel his arm being torn out of the socket and the grip was like a vice. He was caught and could do nothing about it.

At the same moment, bamfoon wobbled up to the Gleek and started to bite savagely at his ear. The Gleek let go of Bobbin and grabbed the bamfoon instead. Bamfoon beckoned for Bobbin to leave. Bobbin did not want to leave his friend but bamfoon kept indicating to him to leave fast. Despairingly, Bobbin left the bamfoon struggling with the ferocious Gleek. Bobbin glanced back once more to see the bamfoon still trapped in the deadly clutches.

Suddenly, an incredible phenomena was unleashed. The same strange forces seemed to be in action as those that had defeated the attack of the great shark. Firstly, there was another underwater explosion with yellow waves, followed rapidly by purple shock waves. And, once more, the bamfoon was suddenly free. He caught up with Bobbin, who was relieved that Nature had timed herself so precisely to help his friend from danger. Bamfoon seemed happy to be alive and showed it by chuckling.

The young princes were glad that Bobbin had accomplished the task he had set himself and, after been supplied with fresh provisions, Bobbin and bamfoon returned to their ship to make sail for Horgan, where they hoped the Wizard of Horgan would interpret the message on the medallion and amulet.

Later, as the ship slowly sailed in the evening quiet,

along coastal routes, it was such a lovely warm night that both friends started to talk about all the places they had seen, and bamfoon told Bobbin of the place where he lived.

'Do you long for your home isle, bamfoon?' The bamfoon smiled, but Bobbin could see it was mingled with sadness and nostalgia. 'We'll sail for your land, bamfoon, before going to Horgan. I wouldn't see you unhappy, dear friend.'

Bamfoon replied, 'You'll not be disappointed in my land, Bobbin. It's a most isolated and lovely island, and very peaceful at all times.'

'What's your land called?'

'It's called Verdandie, and it is surrounded by beautiful palm trees.'

'Well, I'll look forward to staying there for a few days until I feel refreshed again!' Then he changed the subject. 'Tell me, bamfoon. How do you always seem to get someone to rescue you every time you're in danger?'

Bamfoon looked surprised at the question. 'Nobody helps me. I help myself. You see all bamfoons have a strong shock system. Our hair produces the yellow explosive shock and our skirt, as you call it, causes the violent purple shock waves. We can repel anything from sharks to gleeks, although it only works under water.

'So you see we bamfoons can be quite formidable at times — when we choose to be! That's why I'm grateful to you for rescuing me from the Patterns of Vexor, for I've no power on land. When that organism is below water it's still like being on land, which made any escape impossible. On, or under water, I have the strength of a thousand power-eels. Bamfoons are gentle creatures and they'll not hurt anyone unless their own lives are threatened.'

Bobbin's jaw fell. He stared in awe at the power of the bamfoon.

'I'm glad to have you on my side!' laughed Bobbin cheerfully.

The ship continued sailing through the quiet of the night, as if floating silently with the tide like a large piece of driftwood, at length leaving the shoreline and the twin peaks of Neptunia behind on the horizon.

A WELL-DESERVED REST

The land where Bamfoon dwelled was on the same course that would eventually take Bobbin to Horgan. For the bamfoon this was the happiest voyage of his life because he was going home to his true love, his friends and relations.

The bamfoon's home island was made up of a large five-mile sandspit circle, with the sea surrounding it. Within this sandspit circle, which was about half a mile wide, lay a tropical lagoon full of all manner of marine life. In the middle of the lagoon was another, smaller island, and that was where the colony of the bamfoons lived. They were fully self-supporting, living on fish and fruit. Being clumsy swimmers, they made boats they could sail on the lagoon and had much larger boats for working on the sea. As they were within a sandspit, they did not need a harbour in which to moor their boats, but kept the larger boats just by the edge of the open sea. An underground stream fed the lagoon making it a freshwater pool.

Chuckling and shouting to his friends in his big booming voice, bamfoon's large face grinned with pleasure as many of his friends came out to see him, exchanging shouts of joy amongst themselves. They all made Bobbin very welcome, and he was treated to a fine meal, while they played musical instruments and wobbled about in a kind of ceremonial dance. Bobbin enjoyed the food and the pleasant surroundings, and then, to his surprise, the bamfoons gave him a beautiful carved whistle as a present.

Blowing through the whistle, Bobbin saw that it had a special effect upon the bamfoons. He had always known beautiful sea-tunes, which were influenced by the whales' songs. He often imagined that he understood these tunes as if they were a part of his own tradition. Now, with this lovely present, it seemed he might charm the sea creatures and even the birds of the air. This whistle definitely had some further connection with his origins. This too concealed perhaps a clue that could bring him closer to his roots... Bobbin thanked his friends enthusiastically for the present.

His friend said, 'There are only about a hundred and fifty of us bamfoons in the world. We are a dying species. For bamfoons can only have one child in all their lifetime. When I get married I hope we can have a child soon, so that I will be able to continue my lineage.' Then he introduced his girlfriend to Bobbin, her name was Casana. The only difference that Bobbin could see between her and the others was that she had very long dark eyelashes.

'Isn't she lovely?' said bamfoon.

'Indeed! The most beautiful bamfoon I've ever seen,' replied Bobbin.

'Are you going to stay with us for a while, Bobbin?'

'I'd like to stay here for a week, since the air here is so refreshing and the food so good.'

'Our island is a bit overcrowded, but if you want you can sleep in the canopy of trees on the sandspit and look

up to the stars as you drift to sleep.'

'I should like that very much,' Bobbin agreed.

That day, Bobbin just relaxed; rambling all over the island and around the perimeter of the sandspit.

A very large coconut palm seemed ideal to make his bed in, so he climbed up the large tree and made himself a little hammock in the canopy of the tree. What he did not know was that a little monkey had decided to sleep in the same spot as well. However, Bobbin did not mind at all sharing with such a friendly little animal, that kept scampering off every two minutes and returning with gifts of dates and fruit.

What a beautiful cool evening it was! Bobbin simply

luxuriated in the idyllic environment and, as each star began to twinkle in the sky, all seemed perfect. A few spots of rain fell and when Bobbin looked at the sky it quickly seemed to become overcast. The monkey shot away to climb up into a more thickly-leaved tree, for he had no wish to get soaked. Bobbin loved sea water but he knew that rain was different — it could bring on colds or even a fever which he did not relish.

From out of the blue bamfoon appeared, coming up the tree, bringing a huge lily-pad that was big enough to cover the whole crown of the palm tree. On seeing this, the little monkey came scurrying back, deciding to sleep underneath the lily-pad alongside Bobbin. It was good to have him back again.

When bamfoon returned to his own island, he left Bobbin and the monkey dry, comfortable and well-provided for. Then came the wild roar of thunder and the bright flashes of fork-tongued lightning, followed by merciless, torrential rain that crashed down upon the lily-pad, cascading on down the tree like a cataract. Running water made the tree look like a fountain. Both Bobbin and the little monkey snuggled close together. Secure, dry and comfortable, the pair listened to the noise of the waterfall flowing and it made a magical song. Later on as the rain ceased, the droplets were still playing their little tunes, as the waves of the ocean murmured like a mermaid might sing a love song to attract a merman. Bobbin was very happy here on this island, and he eventually stayed for over a month before he realised that he had almost forgotten his main purpose — to find his own identity.

One day, therefore, he gathered his belongings and started to make ready his ship. He was taking on board new provisions and fresh water when bamfoon came rushing up to him and said, 'Bobbin, you weren't going to go away without me were you?'

Bobbin looked surprised. 'But I thought you were very happy in your homeland and you'd be glad to see me on my way!'

'Bobbin, you're my dearest friend! I've never enjoyed myself so much in my life as I have with you. Please — take me with you again.'

'But what about your friends and your girlfriend?'

'I'm still too young to marry, but I've told Casana that we shall marry later, and I've gone through all my tearful farewells to everyone on the island — I want to seek more adventures with you.'

'Then indeed you shall! I've enjoyed your company too — and you've saved my life twice — so, 'Welcome aboard'...'

But there was another visitor in the ship — Monkey. He had decided that he would go voyaging with his new-found friend and no matter how much Bobbin tried to catch him and put him ashore, the monkey just climbed up the mast or spars and ran everywhere about the ship.

'It's no use Bobbin!' cried bamfoon. 'It seems that you're stuck with both of us.'

'Then set sail for Horgan! It's a long journey, let's hope the winds will be in our favour.'

'Aye, aye captain,' chuckled bamfoon as he saluted Bobbin. The little monkey, realising he was firmly aboard as a passenger, jumped from one of the high stays to land on Bobbin's shoulder. Looking sideways toward his shoulder, Bobbin just grinned and said, 'You're a wise and cheeky monkey...'

At that it chattered and scampered all over the ship and seemed to be enjoying all the fun of sailing.

TERRIBLE FUNGUS

The return journey to Horgan became hazardous when the winds turned severe, and the rudder of the ship was damaged.

While Bobbin and the bamfoon were able to fix it once the winds died down, it was not a pleasant job to do because the ship had drifted into a very peculiar slimy sea. Thick green and brown slime made their task difficult, and many kinds of slithering eels and other biting fish nipped at their legs. bamfoon and Bobbin had to put guards around their legs, making the chore more difficult. Eventually they did manage to accomplish the job and the rudder worked once more.

However, an even greater task lay before them — to get the ship back into the open sea and on course for Horgan. These thick weeds and other clinging seaweeds were everywhere. It was as if the seaweed was pulling their ship right into some form of heart to this tangled labyrinth of green slime. Nothing seemed to help them to get back to the open channels of the sea. They were being firmly held by a mass of weed.

A few hundred yards away from them loomed a white-looking island.

'I wonder what lies on that island in the middle of such a terrible masses of slime?' asked bamfoon.

'Well, perhaps it may show us a way out of it. Look at those white trees. If I climb up one I may be able to see the way back to the open sea,' Bobbin said.

'You'd better be very careful, because we don't know what lies upon that island. I've never seen such a white island before. I wonder what makes it so white?'

Bobbin looked at the monkey, who was sitting high up in the rigging, and he noticed that it did not attempt to try and get on the island, even though they were so close that it would just be a case of jumping onto it.

'Strange!' said Bobbin. 'Monkeys are naturally excited by trees and their inquisitive nature usually makes them scamper up to the top of any of them, but for some reason our monkey is not being attracted to these ones.'

Their ship had now ground to a halt, being completely stuck in this mass of weeds and slime. Everything in the sea was so green yet everything on the land was so white. Still the monkey contented itself by staying in the boat.

'Perhaps he knows something that I don't,' Bobbin thought to himself. 'I want you, bamfoon, to stay on the ship and I'll go and explore this island to see if I can find some means of escaping out of these dense weeds.'

Only Bobbin therefore jumped out of the ship and onto the island. A foul smell emanated from the soft white splashy earth. The stench was sickening and almost made Bobbin vomit. Now Bobbin was accustomed to most of the smells of the sea but this vile stench was like nothing he had ever smelt before. Apart from the horrible smell, the earth was soft and marsh-like.

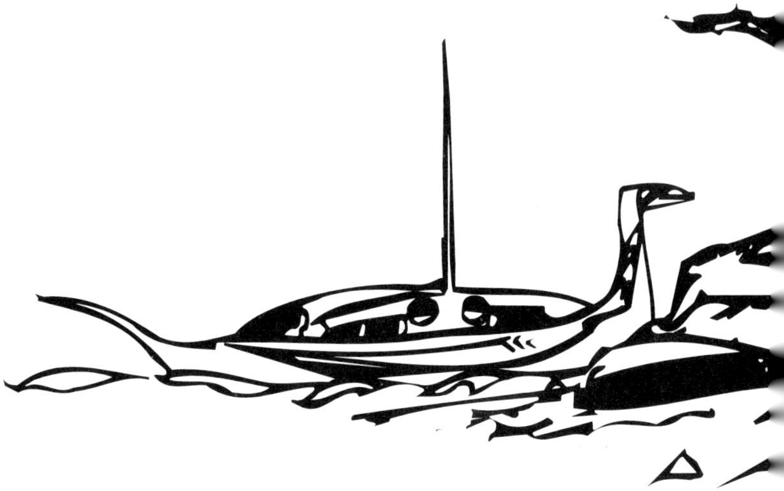

With every step that Bobbin took he felt he was being watched, or as if there was some great danger waiting. He came to one of the tall, white and strange species of tree that he had never seen the likes of before, and he ventured to climb it. But this was no easy tree to climb. The thick white substance that covered everything on the island soon covered Bobbin's hands and nipped at them and the smell became even more repugnant. It was no ordinary task. Every part of his body was aching with the foul white substance and his eyes streamed with tears. But, after a very arduous climb, he did reach the top of this sickly tree, from where Bobbin could see that about ha!f a mile away lay the open sea, clear of weed. The task to release the ship from the grasp of this island and the massing seaweed would not be an easy one.

Climbing down the tree Bobbin slipped. He fell down very fast, pulling a lot of the white substance from the

tree with him. The ground was soft and splashy so he had a soft landing, and he realised then that these were not white trees at all, but just ordinary green trees that had been covered over by a creeping fungus. He then realised that it was imperative to get the ship out of this danger zone very quickly.

Returning to the ship and reporting his findings, Bobbin told the bamfoon, 'The water is too deep and dangerous for us to spend much time trying to release the ship — there are too many thick weeds that will try to trap us, and biting eels to torture us. Yet we're in enormous danger if we can't get out of this place because the fungus will gradually overcome us. I don't know what to do! This is a very perilous time and this situation is utterly precarious.'

'Look over here, Bobbin!' cried the bamfoon. 'That creeping fungus is already beginning to climb onto the deck of the ship. What can we do to prevent it from coming right over the ship?'

Bobbin went below to fetch the stiff bristled brushes for scrubbing the decks and he handed one to the bamfoon saying, 'Keep scrubbing it over the sides of the ship or it will start attacking us as well.'

Both of them worked very hard to scrub the fungus from the deck until they were dog-tired. By the time night fell the pair were completely exhausted and fell asleep, hoping to regain enough strength soon to fight this evil fungus.

But morning found them in a worse situation, for the fungus had by now come right over the ship and Bobbin's feet and hands were covered with the stuff. It was terrifying. Never before had Bobbin encountered such an enemy. Monkey climbed right to the top of the ship. Bamfoon noticed that the white fungus was starting to climb the stays, seemingly after Monkey. The monkey saw it and scampered all over the ship to find the safety of some other rope which the fungus had not yet reached.

Bobbin had left the whistle on the other side of the deck. The fungus was reaching for it when Bobbin ran over and threw it over to another part of the ship where it landed on a ledge. Monkey, attracted by the whistle, scampered down for it. He put it to his mouth and started to blow at it, aping what he had seen Bobbin do many a time.

Strange chilly music emerged from that whistle, causing the most weird and wonderful thing to happen.

The ship swayed violently. This time, however, it was not bamfoon causing one of his underwater shock-waves, but some external eruption. From out of the water there came a huge sea-denison, about forty feet high. He towered above them, while they gazed up at him terrified.

Monkey hid himself under a canvas on the ship as, coming toward the bow of the ship, this huge man-like creature placed both his webbed hands around the bow and carried the ship along the sea of slime and weeds and then out into an open channel. Bamfoon and Bobbin could only gaze, dumbstruck, and wonder why this huge denison should be assisting them, taking them out of the seaweed and fungus. What a great relief it was to be led out and to smell the open briny once more.

It was the whistle. Yes! Something about the whistle summoned this creature from out of his depths of the sea in order to come to their aid, for surely they would have perished if they had remained in that place much longer.

The giant creature waved goodbye and dived back to his home deep under the sea. Bobbin and bamfoon along with the monkey, breathed a sigh of relief. At last they could continue on their journey to Horgan.

Now they knew that the whistle had tremendous powers and the monkey, through some lucky chance, had summoned the great creature up from the deeps. The whistle had the power to call for help when required, and Bobbin must now try to understand the notes of the whistle.

The rest of their journey to Horgan was plain-sailing, and when at last they reached the island, Bobbin and the Bamfoon were full of relief, knowing that they could sleep in safety and that the horror and terror of the green slimy sea of weeds and the island of fungus were far behind them.

HORGAN REVISITED

The rocks of Horgan could be seen easily from afar and its splendid marble castle shone like a jewel in the sun.

Bobbin was no stranger to Horgan and the events of his last visit with King Jack passed through his mind as he approached once more. For it was on Horgan that they had opposed the evil sub-man, Boorg, and finally managed to restore the rightful Wizard of Horgan to the post of King's adviser.

Many memories ran through Bobbin's mind as he looked at this sweet, fruitful side of the island, which was in such sharp contrast to the other, distant rocky part. Nevertheless, in all it was a wonderously beautiful place. The people no longer had to hide underground as they had to before the time when Bobbin flooded the spouting mound of sulphur, which had never erupted again.

The harbour was a small stone-built one, with a difficult entrance. With the help of bamfoon they negotiated it and moored the ship. They had reached another milestone on the voyage and knew that Bobbin was coming nearer to an understanding of his own identity.

They had no sooner docked than a large group of King Yorgo's attendants arrived to welcome them to Horgan. As custom demanded, a new wardrobe of clothes were presented to both the travellers. What a different reception it was from the first one that Bobbin and Jack had received in Horgan when King Yorgo had been so deeply under the spell of the evil Boorg! The young ruler had long since repented his former haughtiness and now he personally arrived with his attendants to meet them.

Bobbin hated robes of state and would have much preferred to wear his ordinary clothes. But tradition demanded that they dress up or they would offend the king's protocol. On the other hand, bamfoon was delighted with the honours being bestowed upon them. He enjoyed putting on clothes of state, for never before in his life had he ever dressed up in such clothes — or any kind of clothes for that matter. It was a new innovation for a bamfoon, who especially liked wearing the turban, on which rich coloured gems were sewn.

All the natives of Horgan remembered Bobbin with kindness and admiration, for he had become a hero on this island. Thanks to Bobbin everyone on Horgan could walk beneath the sun without fear of the mound erupting anymore. Bamfoon was a complete novelty to them. Maybe he was strange-looking, but the folks took an instant liking to this unusual creature. When bamfoon chuckled and sang in his booming voice it caused a stir amongst the natives, who drew him close to their hearts. The feeling was mutual, and bamfoon was delighted with his popularity.

On that very night, there was a feast held in their honour

and all the dignitaries of the land took part, while the poorer subjects received a special bonus from King Yorgo so that they might dance and feast. All the people of the island joined in celebration and remembrance of the freedom of the island won from the evil submen.

No expense was spared. The feast was lavish with the finest of wines and meats for the meal. Speeches were made and all the customs and traditions were observed. Bobbin hated every minute of the fuss! Bamfoon meantime was beside himself with pleasure.

After the speeches, Bobbin had to give an up-to-date account of all that had transpired since their last meeting at King Jack's wedding. Bobbin conveyed love and salu-

tations from his friend and much time passed simply speaking about old times.

The Wizard of Horgan gave a lengthy speech on everything, from magic to the happenings of the land. Bamfoon laughed because he loved everything on Horgan — including the long-winded speeches of the wizard. Bobbin would rather have fought with the Gleek again than have been made to suffer any more of these formal traditions of state.

The night eventually came to an end when everyone had drunk so much and stuffed themselves so fully with food that they had to retire to their beds. Bobbin thought he would go back and sleep on the ship and change out of his uncomfortable robes, but Yorgo insisted that they stay the night in the comfort of the royal palace. Bobbin was disappointed, but he had to grin and bear it. The two friends were given a wonderful room to share and the beds seemed the essence of comfort, with sheets of the finest silk. For Bobbin, it was another cumbersome duty to be to endured. It was all too much for him, especially when bamfoon said, 'Doesn't the time pass by so quickly when you're enjoying yourself totally? This is the very best place I've ever been. Everyone's so friendly.'

Bobbin just had to agree. He was glad that the bamfoon was enjoying it all, even if to him it was all a terrible endurance test.

There was an ornamental pool in their bedroom and some terrapins swimming about in it. Bamfoon had the time of his life wearing his clothes, and admiring himself in the mirrors.

'What a soft feather bed!' cried the bamfoon.

Bobbin moaned, 'Well, I'm not going to lie in it.' He took off all his clothes and going into the shallow pool, said, 'I'm more comfortable sharing a bed with terrapins.' And there he settled down for the night and fell sound asleep.

Morning light woke the two friends. Bamfoon had had an excellent night's sleep and was in the very best of spirits, but not so Bobbin. He tried to be cheerful, but his heart was downcast, until his pet monkey, who had remained on the ship, suddenly startled them by darting in, running straight up to Bobbin's face. Bobbin felt a bit better then, the monkey's antics were so funny that his spirits rose.

Today he would meet with the old Wizard of Horgan, and Bobbin hoped that he would learn a bit more about himself.

After waiting an hour outside the castle, the wizard appeared. 'I'm sorry I'm late, but there were some most important points I had to make to the king at the council meeting... Never mind! I am free now to discuss with you whatever it is you want to know.'

The bamfoon said that he wanted to go for a walk with the monkey, and he also needed to find some provisions for the ship.

Taking out the medallion and the amulet, Bobbin showed them to the wizard, asking him what language they might be written in and what they said. With an interested look the old Wizard took the pieces in his hands and studied the inscription.

'Ah! This, my dear Bobbin, is in the language of the ancient Delphinians and it contains a message in its verse. It is a salt-sea sonnet and the words read as follows:

Where the sea is blue and deep,
Where the brown shark lies asleep.

By the coral's golden sand,
Echoes to another land.
Further down below the fish,
The road leads to promise wish.

There you find the very best,
Answer to your humble quest.

Bobbin was struck by the unusual nature of the verse.

The Wizard went on, 'This salt-sea sonnet is obviously a chart to let you know which direction to take in your quest to find your true identity. I think there is probably some deep blue hole in the sea — under a coral reef — where a passageway would take you further down still. A land must surely be there beneath the waves, but it is so secretly concealed that it could prove extremely difficult to locate. Find that special passageway under the sea!

'The only real clue that you have is within the part of the salt-sea sonnet where it mentions the brown sharks lying asleep. I know of many spots where sharks are to be found, but you will have to explore every one of them. This will be a very time-consuming business: perhaps — yes — perhaps I can help you in a more practical manner by using my magic powers to locate this hidden place...

'You see, Bobbin, Delphinia is an underwater civilisation, and the inhabitants there are a very intelligent people. Very few mariners have ever found the place because it is so deep down below the surface of the sea. Stories have been told of sailors drowning and then falling right down to the ocean bed where they are picked up by Delphinians and brought back to health. Usually these sailors are sent back to the surface to be picked up by passing ships, for the Delphinians are kind but mysterious people. I have a feeling, my dear boy, it is of utmost importance that you should reach Delphinia as soon as possible. To make sure that you understand a little about yourself and your origin I'll show you my own pool of wisdom, and if you still have your special whistle then I shall be able to conjure up a vision for you...'

The Wizard of Horgan was a very long-winded man, but he did have great knowledge of things.

Bobbin answered, 'I do have my whistle and I do appreciate very much your help. Without your assistance I may never find the secret of my beginnings.'

'Then indeed you shall be enlightened. Just follow me to my own cave at the other side of Horgan, where I shall summon up the help and knowledge you need.'

The wizard, talking all the while, took Bobbin along the road to the other side of Horgan where there was a concealed cave among the rocks.

'This is my own cave, you see, Bobbin, where I do a lot of my magic spells and it is in here that I have my pool. Since the spell I am going to do is for you, I shall need to play a few notes on your whistle. I know how to work the pool and I shall ask the questions on your behalf, in order that we both may see the answers in the form of a vision, but — you must be ready to face anything that you see or find out.'

'I'm prepared for whatever I may find,' replied Bobbin.

So the old wizard then played a few notes on Bobbin's whistle... and a blue mist rose to encircle them both. It was a cool mist, while the sounds of dolphins singing were heard within the cave and their high-pitched noises seemed loud enough to penetrate right through their heads. When the mists cleared the pool looked very clear and enticing.

'We may have to wait a few moments now until the spell starts working,' muttered the old wizard.

A fine scent emerged from the pool, like the aroma of fresh garden flowers and the fragrance became prevalent all round the cave. The pool swirled gently with small ripples and eddies and then Bobbin felt he was being drawn by a magnetic force, right into the pool. He looked around quickly for the wizard but he seemed to be alone.

The vision commenced with a scene inside a most splendid palace. A beautiful girl, with long blonde hair, was standing by an opening to a passage that appeared to be secret. She was dressed in the most richly-textured apparel that Bobbin had ever seen. Her eyes were wet with tears and she wore a sad expression on her face. She was holding two silver boxes, both of which were closed. Around her neck was a jewelled necklace, and a medallion and amulet that Bobbin recognized instantly. With great sadness she carried both the small silver boxes into the secret passage and across a gloomy cave to a strange-looking tube at the far end, in which she placed both boxes and then quickly shut the porthole-like door to the tube. Within seconds this tube filled up with sea water and the boxes were swept away upwards towards the open sea — far above where she stood, alone and sad.

Bobbin could observe the boxes going up the tube and he knew instinctively that he was one of the children within those boxes. Remembering what his earthly mother had told him before he went away, it was clear to him now that this sad lady was his real mother and that Maera was the child in the second silver box and and that she was also his real sister.

So it was that, looking at the beautiful lady whom he knew now to be his mother, he could not help but feel deeply disturbed. Tears flowed down his cheeks, because at last he had discovered that he belonged once to a mother who for some powerful reason had to abandon him and his sister. There was no way he could know what her motives might be for such an action, but he could see that she was deeply distressed. Only a few inches seemed to separate them. Bobbin reached to touch his mother in the vision... when, all of a sudden, he was back in the Wizard of Horgan's cave.

'Ugh! That was silly of you, Bobbin,' cried the old wizard. 'You must never touch anything in a vision or it just closes up on you!'

'I—I couldn't help myself — it was so real and so close,' he said sadly.

'Well, now that the vision has closed up perhaps I can still tell you a little about the things that I saw because, simultaneously to your vision, I was able to go somewhere else in the land of Delphinia.

The lady whom you saw was none other than your real mother but what you do not know is that she is a princess of Delphinia and also a high priestess of the sea. It is forbidden for a priestess to marry. As I was able to look into a very different time from you, I saw another part of her life: I saw her when she was acting as a priestess of the sea and I saw her life unfolding. Very stupidly she married a man from another place without letting her father the king know. As it was forbidden, she kept it secret until your father left her, and by then she was expecting a baby. When she was delivered, twins were born. You are right — Maera is your sister, which is why you have always felt so close to her. Your father was summoned to another place and I was unable to see him in the vision, but I did see your mother being found out and the penalty was that she was to be banished to a far away isle in the Southern Ocean. Where that is I cannot tell. Only your grandfather knows where she was to be banished to.

'To free your mother from her prison isle, you will have to journey to find Delphinia on your own. It will mean trying all the deep blue holes and going where the brown sharks lie asleep, which as you know is a mystery because sharks drown if ever they stop moving. All the signs seem to be within the salt-sea sonnet. If you hadn't touched your mother in the vision I might have found out who exactly your father is and why he had to leave your mother. To where he was summoned, and why, are presently two great puzzles to us. I am sorry, Bobbin, I cannot help you any more.'

Bobbin thanked the Wizard of Horgan for his help.

Once more Bobbin set sail to find out more about his parents, and bamfoon and the monkey journeyed with him. At least Bobbin had found out much more than he knew before. Now he must put into practise the words of wisdom contained within the salt-sea sonnet.

BLUE HOLES

Thousands of deep blue holes were scattered around the oceans, giving Bobbin a tricky problem.

They stopped at countless blue holes, but if they noticed sharks swimming around any of them they never ventured down, because the sonnet told them that the deep blue hole was where there were sleeping brown sharks. Both Bobbin and bamfoon already knew of many such blue holes, but they especially wanted one near to a coral reef and close beside golden sands. Six times Bobbin dived down toward likely blue holes, but to no avail, for the currents were treacherous and they were dangerously deep. Sometimes bamfoon made Bobbin tie a cord around him and the other end bamfoon secured to the side of the boat. Giant squids were known to frequent these deep places and each dive was perilous.

After six dives in a row proved fruitless, the bamfoon suddenly remembered an isolated desert island where he thought a massive coral reef existed, and where a deep blue hole lay near to golden sands. Although he had only

seen it once when he was very young, it was his father whom he now remembered telling him of it. With excitement, bamfoon told Bobbin all he knew and they immediately sailed towards the south in order to locate this special blue hole. Bobbin felt within his heart that this time he would surely find the place mentioned in the salt-sea sonnet.

Two days of hard sailing took them to the place. Everything was there: the blue hole, the coral reef and the golden sand of the nearby island. Bobbin's eyes lit up. He was filled with excitement. He might be on the verge of discovering his real grandfather, the King of Delphinia...

Bamfoon cautioned Bobbin to be extra careful when passing the sleeping sharks, he knew that although they

might be still they would be very dangerous if awakened suddenly. Bobbin was recklessly afraid of nothing at this time — his mind was completely bent on his goal.

Armed only with his knife, Bobbin dived straight into the deep blue hole. It was clear as crystal down below, but he had to swim hard against a very strong current and the descent was long and exhausting.

After a struggle against the sea he finally made out the bottom of the ocean bed and, looking around, could see a large coral reef rising nearby. Fish of every description were swimming in and out of the flow of the current and large anemones were stretching forth their tentacles in search of food. Everywhere there were huge splits in the coral reef, probably caused by underwater earthquakes. This made Bobbin's task even more difficult, for a choice had to be made as to which chasm would be the right one. Yet the words of the salt-sea sonnet said quite a bit about sleeping sharks, so Bobbin persevered further along the great reef until, in the distance, he could see hundreds of brown, sleeping sharks. At last he felt that he must now be near to the secret entrance to Delphinia.

Bobbin approached a large split in the wall of the reef which he entered cautiously. Inside it grew darker and darker, but Bobbin could not allow himself to be frightened. Along this narrow passageway he swam until at last he came to the surface within a large underground cave. All around were many eels, some in the water and some on the dry rock. They were no threat to him, being more frightened of Bobbin's presence than anything else. The lad sighed with relief that he had made it at long last.

Seeing a pathway running from the cave and going even further down into the depths of the earth, Bobbin realised soon that more of the salt-sea sonnet was now coming to light. For all around him, his path was lightened by a green luminous substance on the walls, so that he could pursue his course secure in the knowledge that he would surely be led to his place of birth.

Weary from his swimming, Bobbin came to a large white door. 'This must be the entrance to Delphinia,' he thought to himself, and approaching, he turned the knob and let himself in.

He was immediately in a perfumed garden, with an array of colours that his eyes feasted on. Bobbin's hair shimmered with amazed excitement.

Troops of Delphinian soldiers, dressed in marvellous uniforms made of fine cloth, came towards Bobbin. They approached him in amazement. Bobbin felt akin to these folk and the large crowd that gathered around him, looking at him closely.

A head soldier spoke, 'You are a stranger here, yet you seem very familiar to us. We must take you to the king, who will see that you want for nothing. I am afraid we are all looking at you so very strangely because we are wondering how it was that you managed to come through the under-earth and sea-gate. Come now to be received by the King.'

King Ragono was a good and just king. Whenever a stranger fell from a ship in his area he would attend to his needs and, when well enough to leave, would put him up to the surface to be picked up by a passing ship. On seeing Bobbin, however, this old king felt the strings of his heart playing a strange melody. He welcomed the young lad with open arms, shedding a tear. This young sea-boy was far too near his own kin for him not to sense a strange wonder. The king knew it with certainty and so did Bobbin.

'I have never seen you before, boy, but you move me in a most paternal way. Whoever are you?'

'I am Bobbin. I am the son of your own daughter, who was banished beyond the beyond. You are my grandfather.'

The old king was speechless. Eventually he spoke, 'I have no quarrel with you, my boy. It is true that your mother did break the laws of Delphinia. She was a high priestess of the sea and married your father against all the laws of this land. I loved my daughter Airiel very much, but I was powerless to change our laws. She had to be banished. But you, my grandson, will be proclaimed a prince of this realm at once and you shall rule after me, here in Delphinia.'

'But I couldn't! Not without trying to redeem my

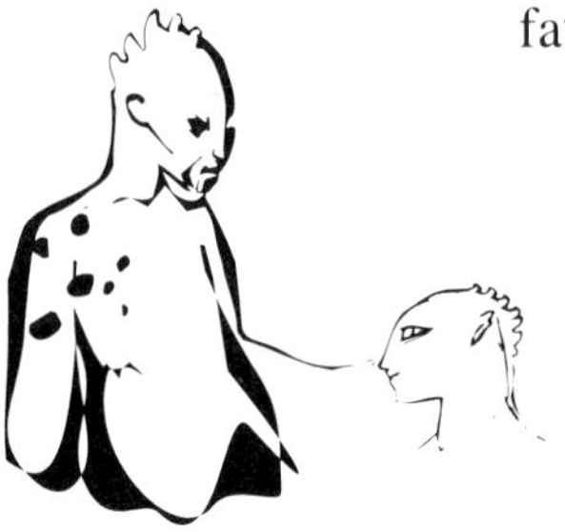

mother and trying to find my true father. Do you know who he is, Grandfather?'

'No, I do not know who he is. Your mother would not tell me. If only she had spoken up then, we could perhaps have negotiated a marriage contract, and she need not have been banished to such an island, far away in the Southern Ocean. And, what puzzled everyone was the fact of how your father — whoever he might have been — found a way into the temple of the sea to have a secret rendevous with her. In fact they must have had many secret meetings and a clandestine marriage ceremony.'

'Then surely he must be a great magician, if he had the powers to enter here and discover her secret chambers,' Bobbin remarked.

'Possibly, but your mother never revealed who he was. For some reason she was protecting him.'

'Grandfather, if I can sail my ship to the island far in the Southern Ocean, would I be permitted to take her somewhere more pleasant?'

'Yes — it is possible — although she was banished there forever. Were she able to escape from that prison island she could then renounce her title of princess and High Priestess, become a commoner, and even return to Delphinia, as a subject. Perhaps then her husband might return and the three of you could be reconciled once more as a family.'

'But, Grandfather, I also have a sister, Maera. She too is part of this family. You would love her too

Grandfather, because she is a truly beautiful girl and very much a Delphinian.'

Another tear streamed down the old king's face. 'It is a very sad business,' he said wearily. 'You would need many provisions for such a journey, and weapons.'

'No,' replied Bobbin. 'I have two trusted companions with me, and they're keeping watch, right at this moment where they await on my ship my return.'

'Then you had better let me tell you how you might try to free my daughter from the prison island, far away in the Southern Ocean...

'Airiel may wander wherever she wants to on the island, but she cannot leave it because of a gold chain. It was especially fashioned to fit forever around her ankle and can only be opened by two keys. Those two keys are to be found on the island, but all I know about how to find them is this! 'if one is beyond your reach, then the other is within your reach'.

'You would need to find both those keys. One of them releases her from the golden chain, but it also lets loose the Scorpra — a huge cobra — with venomous fangs, and a scorpion's sting. It is ferocious. Nobody has ever escaped from the island within living history. However it is supposed not to swim too far, for it's a land monster. Remember then, that though the two keys can grant freedom, they could also mean death for all of you. I wish you the very best of luck, Bobbin, but I would far rather you stayed here.'

'I must find out my true origins, Grandfather. I have only half my quest fulfilled, therefore I have to find the other half of me.'

Bobbin kissed his grandfather goodbye.

'Bobbin, leave through one of the secret entrances — only known to us.'

Bobbin was escorted by the soldiers to the door to a tunnel, which he entered. Water then filled the tunnel behind and beneath him, and suddenly and with great force he was pushed right up through the passage at high speed and thrown clear out from beneath the sea to nearly fifty feet above the waves.

The bamfoon, standing on the deck of the ship, saw in the distance an object shooting out of the water. Only minutes later Bobbin appeared back on board to tell of his adventure. Monkey hopped and swung excitedly. As Bobbin told them about his mother and the meeting with his grandfather and the welcome he had received in Delphinia, bamfoon sat enthralled.

'You must realise, though,' said Bobbin, 'that this prison island adventure will be very dangerous. So I expect you both to stay in the ship and, if I am killed by the Scorpra, you must sail the ship away back to your own lands.'

Bamfoon turned red with rage, 'How dare you even think of leaving me behind on a ship! I love this adventure. This is the most thrilling time I've ever had. So, you can forget about leaving me behind on any ship!'

The monkey, looking playfully at them both as if he knew what they were saying, took up a stick from the deck and bopped Bobbin over the head with it as if he were sharing the very same sentiments as bamfoon.

'We three make a great team!' cried bamfoon, chuckling and laughing with his loud assuring voice. 'So — it's set sail for the great Southern Ocean, Captain!'

'Southern Ocean, here we come!' cried Bobbin as off they set once more.

PRISON ISLAND

Gigantic waves battered the sides of the ship during the voyage south to the island in the great Southern Ocean. Monkey kept well inside the hull of the ship in fear that he might be swept away by such mountainous waves, while bamfoon and Bobbin continually steered the ship preventing her from straying from her proper course. Although the journey was only three days away from Delphinia, they had already been on a southerly course for three days, and the weather remained very stormy.

On the third day the storms abated and a more agreeable wind hurried them along to complete their journey to the island. Bobbin was surprised to find that the island was quite minute — he could see only a small straw-roofed dwelling, and one enormous tree. The top of it seemed to glitter in the sun. As they drew closer they could see more of the island, and small woods where sea birds nested. The whole place seemed pleasant — if only it were not for the fact that it was being used a prison for Princess Airiel.

Bamfoon was worried about what else they might find on the island, for all of them were aware of the Scorpra's presence and knew that danger lay in store. Carefully they steered their ship to a quiet inlet, where they took to the small rowing boat.

As they rowed in, Bobbin noticed a beautiful lady walking along the sands of the beach; she appeared to be looking at shells on the shore. The monkey carried Bobbin's whistle. He liked to blow upon it every two minutes, which always made bamfoon chuckle.

The lady walking on the shore spotted the visitors and hastily ran to see who the new arrivals might be. It had been years since she had seen another face. Arriving at the spot where the rowing boat came to shore she stopped to gaze at the sea-boy, with a monkey and the strange-looking bamfoon.

'Please, do not be alarmed!' shouted Bobbin, reassuring her that they were friendly. Bamfoon chuckled with joy, while Monkey jumped ashore at once and scampered off to and fro on the island.

Bamfoon wandered off after him to see what mischief he might be up to.

Airiel looked very wonderingly at Bobbin and asked, 'Who are you, young man?'

Bobbin replied, 'I am your son, and everyone calls me Bobbin.'

Airiel held out her arms to Bobbin. 'Come to my arms, Bobbin, and let me kiss you. You cannot imagine how many times I have thought about you. Come quickly before I waken from my dream.'

'I am not a figment of your imagination, Mother. I am real. Touch me and see. I too have waited with great patience to meet you, Mother.'

They both embraced in a tearful hug. Not a word was

spoken for five minutes.

'Mother — I know also where my sister Maera lives. She looks like you! Maera is lady-in-waiting to Beltarra, the wife of King Jack. She's happy there but, like me, she yearns to find out about her past, so when we help you escape from this forsaken lonely island, I'll reunite you with your daughter!'

'That would fulfil all my dreams,' replied Airiel. 'But — at last — I've found you!'

Bamfoon returned and Bobbin introduced him to his mother. Then Airiel made a fine feast from the simple things she had picked from around the island. She was so happy sharing her dwelling with her son and his companions, who sat round the fire telling stories all night so that she caught up with some of Bobbin's adventures. 'Tomorrow,' he said, 'we shall make plans for your escape, and take you home to Delphinia where your father will forgive you and you'll be free to become a loyal subject.'

Sadly she looked at the golden ring, securely fastened around her ankle, although there was no chain to be seen. 'Tomorrow, Mother, we'll find the key that sets you free. Your father has told us of the Scorpra, and we can arrange suitable plans for your escape. Speed must be the secret for our flight from this island. Granfather told me that there are two keys that must be found to release you from that invisible gold chain attached to your ankle. And he also said that one key is out of reach — but the other within our reach... It is a bit puzzling to me, that bit, but I'm sure we'll discover the answer in the morning.'

Airiel then said, 'I've never seen the Scorpra, Bobbin. He'll only come if the lock on my ankle is broken.'

'Well, Mother, on the way here we saw a very lofty

tree. It must have been the tallest on the island and, even at a distance, the top seemed to glitter in the sun. Don't you think that glitter could come from the keys which lies 'not within our reach'? If that's so then I'm sure we can devise a way to retrieve it. I don't know where to look for the other key though, and both keys must be found before you can be set free.'

Bamfoon yawned, 'I think I'll try to get some sleep,' he said.

'Yes, we could all do with a good night's sleep,' Bobbin agreed. 'But first — may I talk to you in private, Mother — on a very delicate matter?'

So it was that mother and son both went for a walk along the moonlit shore. It was beautiful. Bobbin picked up the courage eventually to ask his mother, 'Who is my father?'

'You've the right to know, Bobbin, who your father is and so truthfully I shall tell you...

'Many years ago, I was priestess to the sea gods, and I used to serve them by means of a large mirror in the temple of the sea. My temple was private and I could not let anyone in without the authority of the King, my father, who trusted me, for I was a good priestess. I had many special powers then.

'One day as I was doing work as priestess, I was on my own, when suddenly a handsome fair young man, very much like yourself, appeared in my room. He must have had great powers to come through my temple mirror, and I knew at once that this extraordinary person was no ordinary man. He said that he'd seen me through the other side of the mirror and that he'd fallen in love wih me.

'I was taken aback. I told him that I was a royal

princess and high priestess of the sea, and that it was strictly forbidden for me to receive any visitors without the consent of my father, the King. That didn't deter him at all. He laughed and replied that he was a sea-god himself, and had the power to come through the mirror at any time he wished, for he was above a law that was meant only for mortals. There was nothing I could do to prevent him coming to see me!

'Every night thereafter he came to see me, and eventually I fell in love with him. He asked me to marry him, secretly, and said that he would get permission from a higher law. So we were married in secret, in my temple of the sea, and I remember there were many guests who came through the mirror to attend to me — I wore the loveliest dress...

'Only my father didn't know of our marriage.

'Each evening, my husband would come to me and bring me fruits from the islands of the world. Always he came through the mirror. Each night I waited on him, and all the while my father assumed that I was in deep devotions in my temple, for he suspected nothing.

'But then one evening your father never returned. My happiness was shattered. Each night I waited on him, but never — oh, never did he return. Then, I found I was going to have a baby. There was no way I could tell my father, so instead I went into a spiritual retreat. Still nobody suspected, as it was common for a priestess to go into a spiritual retreat. During my retreat I received no visitors — not even my father was allowed to visit me. It was during that time that I made those inscriptions on your amulet and medallion. They were all to be left as a legacy for you, my child. Then, I was delivered of twins. I had to share the legacy between you...

'How it hurt... to send you both away in the silver boxes and cast you away in the shutes towards the sea... All I could do was hope that you both would be picked up, and the treasures enclosed with each of you would secure you a home.

'Time passed and eventually I had to tell the truth to my father. I had to confess all to him, because I had by that time lost the powers of a priestess. By my actions I had forfeited all my rights to be a princess as well. He asked me to reveal the name of the man who was the father of my children, but I simply couldn't divulge that to him...

'My punishment was banishment here — to this island.'

Bobbin waited quietly for a moment before saying very gently, 'Who, then, is my father?'

Airiel brightened suddenly, 'Your father is a wonderful, handsome sea-god called Sealron. You'd better hold onto your hat when I tell you who he really is! My husband — your real father — is the youngest son of the great Oceanius himself — the most powerful of all the sea-gods!'

Bobbin was taken aback. To know that on one side he had a King of Delphinia as his maternal grandfather, and now, on the other, his paternal grandfather was the greatly feared sea-god Oceanius left Bobbin dumb.

'I'm stunned!' he said. 'But — I cannot understand — why did my father forsake you?'

'He never forsook me! I think he was called upon by his father, and that he's been away on the other side of the world doing work whilst unaware of my plight.

Perhaps he even returned through the mirror several times but I was not there. Maybe he's looking for me at this very moment... You see, Bobbin, no matter what anyone says, I'm his legal and sea-lawful wife; just as you are his son and Maera his daughter...'

'Mother, I shall get you off this island and I shall find the two keys, whatever may come. One day we shall all be reunited...'

Together they returned to the dwelling.

Next morning they rose early to put together all their ideas about where the keys might be. After all their channels of thought had been discussed, they felt able to embark upon the best of the plans they could think of.

Bobbin thought that the key 'out of reach' would be something to do with the golden glitterings on the top of the high tree. This was where they went first.

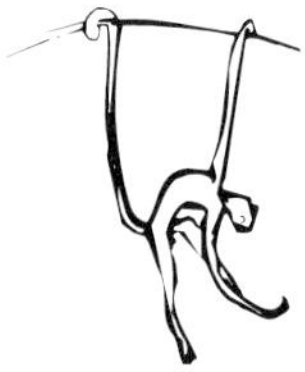

Bobbin attempted to climb up the tree but it had a slippery resin all over it. This posed a big problem to them until Monkey scampered away up the tree, the resin causing him no problem. He climbed right up to the very top and there indeed was the golden key! Monkey grabbed it and broke it loose, and just as rapidly scampered back down with the key in his mouth.

'We dare not try to open the lock yet,' cried Bobbin, 'until we've found the other key 'within our reach'.'

Excitedly, Airiel calls to everyone, 'It's probably right under our very noses, but we cannot pick it up. Let's look all around our feet because it's supposed to be within our reach.'

They searched the rest of the morning without luck and had come almost to despair when suddenly Bamfoon cried out in his big booming voice, 'I've got it! It's just struck me! How foolish we all are. We're all looking at our feet for the key — when it's already 'within our reach'. It's not a physical key — for that's the one Monkey retrieved from the top of the tree — it's a musical key!

'Bobbin, you've got the whistle: if that first key was the very top one, because of the tree, then the other key must be the very lowest notes on the scales of your whistle. First we'd to 'ascend the scale for the top key', now we've 'to descend the scale to find the bottom key'.'

Bobbin yelled out in triumph, 'I think you've solved it, bamfoon — Well done!'

They hurried back to the rowing boat, where Bobbin took the whistle, while the other key remained ready in bamfoon's hands so they could hurry away once the lock was broken.

'Have everything in readiness,' cried Bobbin, and as they stood on the shore fully prepared, he put the whistle to his lips, playing the very lowest notes upon it. A very shrill and loud scream was heard as with speed the bamfoon unlocked and opened the golden chain around Airiel's ankle, and all ran for the rowing boat. The ground shook, and suddenly, right behind them, there burst out of the earth the monstrous Scorpra. With terrible blood-curdling growls it came for them. Never had Bobbin rowed so hard, he was rowing for their lives. He knew that if only he were alone he could have swum away to safety, but just now he was desperately frightened for his mother...

A strong current made the rowing difficult and hindered Bobbin. Scorpra was gaining on them. 'We shall have to get out and fight in the water,' yelled Bobbin.

'No!' cried the bamfoon. 'Row your mother and the monkey to the safety of the ship! I'll go into the water with the Scorpra.' Without another word, bamfoon dived into the water. Bobbin realised that the bamfoon was risking his own life to save them, but he could only row feverishly until they reached the ship and boarded it. At last they were safe.

Bamfoon was alone, swimming clumsily in the high waves and inevitably the mighty Scorpra bore down on him. The friends on the ship could only watch with horror as they saw bamfoon tackle the Scorpra.

Spitting and lashing with venom, the Scorpra was trying its best to kill bamfoon. The bamfoon meanwhile gave out constant yellow waves followed by purple shock waves. They did not seem to stop the monster. Bobbin watched helplessly — then he saw something that he had never seen before.

The bamfoon raised himself right onto the top of the waves before emitting an evil and powerful black wave which was so strong that the very ship quaked with the power of it. Its blast rocked the Scorpra, making him stagger and then turn to stumble towards the shore; but the bamfoon was in bad trouble. He could hardly move in the water, and Bobbin dived in at once for his friend.

Bringing the bamfoon back on board they found him very sick and weak. Using all his power to save his friends' lives, bamfoon was now at death's door. Bobbin cried for his dear and wonderful friend. 'Please do not die! I'll find whatever you need to heal you.'

Bamfoon smiled, gently, 'I do not mind dying now... now that I know you're safe...'

Airiel, however, was staring amazed at Bobbin's whistle, 'That's your father's whistle! Give it to me, quick!' she cried. 'He showed me the notes and the incantation which is the other part of your salt-sea sonnet for summoning him if ever I needed him, and now — surely — is that time!'

She put the whistle to her mouth and played a strange little tune, after which she sang the twin half to the salt-sea sonnet:

From the land beyond the deep
Or by the cliffs that hang so steep,
Or in the caves where rock bats fly,
Ascending where the rain clouds sigh,
In twilight worlds or nightly shades,
Gliding o'er the everglades,
No matter what the time of year,
I bid you, Sealron, now appear.

Around them, all the while, the air turned chilly and the waves started to swell. From out of the blue haze came a fantastic sea-carriage, sweeping straight towards them. The doors opened and out came the handsome Sealron. He looked magnificent. With a mighty leap he landed right on board beside his wife. He kissed and embraced her passionately, crying, 'Where have you been, dear Airiel! I tried so many times to come through your mirror, but you were never there...' Airiel wept. 'For a season I was summoned by my father to go and attend to the problems of the sea at the other side of the world, but I did return for you!'

Quickly, she related the main story to Sealron. Then he picked up Bobbin and cuddled him close to his bosom. 'None of you will ever leave my side again! I have many powers and I'll take you all home with me now. We shall collect my daughter, Maera, as well.'

'But please, Father, couldn't you help my friend, bamfoon, who seems to have lost his life so that we could be saved.'

Sealron went over to the bamfoon, saying, 'Well, bamfoon, I hear you've given your black shock wave to save your friends. I know this for you is like the sting of bee, and that once a bamfoon gives a black shock wave it must die, for it has spent its ultimate defence. I shall not let you die, however. I shall return your black shock wave to you once more.'

Sealron ordered everyone to stay back. He touched the bamfoon's head and produced a powerful black shock. Moments later bamfoon sat up, chuckling.

'My son,' cried Sealron, turning to Bobbin, 'I often felt that I may have had a son, so I left you clues all over the seas. The sea-sweets I left with the Sea-Oracle as I knew that a son of mine would go to seek her knowledge. I knew too that it would be very natural to follow from the Sea-Oracle to the Green Man of Positive-thinking, and I'm afraid there is usually a poor bamfoon captured by the Patterns of Vexors, so I felt that if I left my whistle on bamfoon island, some day, sooner or later, my son would come along and find it.

'The whistle, as you know, has the power to summon up help and assistance when needed, and,' he said, smiling, 'it also communicates between my wife and me. Even the sons of Neptune were warned in advance never to hurt anyone that may even resemble me on peril of their lives. All the sea-creatures would know who you are. Only the sharks are treacherous.

'The bamfoon has been a wonderful friend to you and so has the monkey. I have much to tell you, Bobbin, and even more to show you. There is a grand inheritance waiting for you.'

'I'm so very happy to have found you, Father, and you, Mother. Now at last I feel I belong.'

'You have a great deal to learn yet, and I have a lot of making up to do for you. I promise that you'll have everything restored to you.'

Sealron took back his whistle and played on it a frisky tune. Within seconds there came up beside the ship a marvellous, sea-green carriage. 'We shall all return to my land, and there I must explain everything to my father. Being the important sea-god, Oceanius, he will tell me what to do. All this will be new to him, so I do not know how he'll react, but I do know he loves me and I feel perfectly happy in telling him that I am married and have a family. Many wanted me to marry the goddess, Casseiopia, but I refused to do it, for my heart already belonged to another.'

They all got into the green sea-carriage, and were whisked away on an underwater voyage.

THE GRAND MEETING

What an exhilirating journey it was! Things went flying past with the speed of light. Bobbin thought surely, his father must have very powerful arts at his command to be able to do such things, and show them the scenes that they saw. The best was yet to come. Bobbin knew that his grandfather was the very mighty sea-god Oceanius and as he thought about what kind of welcome they would receive, his mind filled with different thoughts; he felt in awe of the glorious scenes that might be yet to come.

The sea-carriage came to a halt at a beautiful palace situated on a sunlit island. It was like Paradise. Flowers were strewn thickly all over the place, tall trees, verdant hills and lush valleys could be seen in all directions. The scene was panoramic and the air fragrantly refreshing.

Sealron took his wife Airiel by the hand, while the rest of the crew followed after them. Bamfoon was a little afraid of meeting the mighty Oceanius, but Monkey seemed unconcerned about what was going on around him and merely sat, amused, on Bobbin's shoulders.

On entering the great palace they saw a huge throne. Sitting upon it was Oceanius himself. His hair was fair and curled. He wore a crown of emeralds and his whole person shone like a star. Servants attended to him — all of them holding him in great respect.

Sealron spoke out, 'Father, I hope you will forgive me for what I have done, since I must now make a confession to you. Some years ago, I secretly married a priestess from Delphinia without the consent of her father. I am fully aware that you decreed I should marry the Princess Cassieopia but I could not find it in my heart to do so, for I loved her not. Instead I have disobeyed by marrying Airiel, the daughter of the king of Delphinia. She stands here with me now, along with one of the two children she bore me in secret.'

Sealron then bowed his head and waited for the sea-god to return his verdict and punishment. Not a word was spoken. Everybody was afraid.

Then Oceanius spoke, 'Do you think that I do not know what you have been up to, Sealron? I know everything that occurs, and most especially when it happens to concern my youngest son!

'From my own pool of thoughts, right here, I long ago saw you secretly enter into the temple of the sea to meet your sweetheart. At first I was angry, but witheld this feeling as I saw you both grew to love each other. So I then recalled you, to see if you would forget Airiel, but you never did. I watched also as Airiel confessed to her father and so lost everything — because of you, my son. She never betrayed you to her father when she could have done so, for by telling her father he could have demanded that his daughter marry you. She has been more than honourable throughout this ordeal. At first I

admired Airiel for her devotion and loyalty, even sacrificing her own happiness and children to save your good name, Sealron. But now I have an even stronger love for Airiel because of what she has endured.

'Bobbin and Maera have never really been in danger. Long ago I endowed them with special gifts, which is why they can swim so well. Every step they have taken since they were born I have guided and protected, because they are my very own kin and destined to be rulers.'

He called for Bobbin to draw near him.

'You, Bobbin, shall therefore judge your father and your mother, not me, and whatever you decide to mete

out to them, so shall it be!'

What a sigh of relief Bobbin gave! 'Please, Sire, it is my judgement that my mother and father be forgiven of any wrong that they've done, and that we shall be united as a family under a bond of love.'

'It is done as you wish, Bobbin. Now, I may embrace all of my family. All come nigh unto me, so that I may embrace you all and give each of you my blessing. You as well, Bamfoon, and you, Monkey.' All ran to touch the great Oceanius. 'My dearest Airiel and Sealron, you shall now have a proper sea-wedding! I now give you both royal approval — let there be a wedding held here, followed by a great feast!'

The gigantic sea-god rose from his throne, a towering figure, and banged his fist on a gong. Straightway, while the echoes boomed and rippled, through his own magic pool came all kinds of guests...

There came the King of Delphinia, the King of Horgan, accompanied by the famous wizard. The King and Queen of Mardaras appeared, and the King and Queen of Gumboria, with Tryeena the witch. Jack and Belltarra walked happily from the magic pool alongside the new princess, Maera, together with Noguila the wisest wizard in all wizardom. Bobbin was excited when he recognized the Queen of the Slinkers come in with her daughter, Balena, who ran at once right up to Bobbin and kissed him, for she thought the world of Bobbin. Then came the Sea-Oracle with the Green Man of Positive-thinking. Everyone there had been a friend or helper to Bobbin on previous occasions. Mistyo and Cloudio, and their father, the great Neptune arrived...

It was truly a feast of feasts. The King of Delphinia had brought a great dowry, and how happily he restored all his blessings on Airiel once more! Now Airiel was one of the most powerful queens in the world. Most of the guests were amazed to be suddenly transported from wherever they had been, straight into this wedding feast. And then, to the surprise of bamfoon, his girlfriend, Casana, and two other bamfoon friends were there too.

It was perfection! Bobbin, who was only fourteen years of age, had accomplished all that he had set out to do. He was at last a whole person and had succeeded in completing his quest to find out who he really was.

There was one special surprise for Bobbin. Oceanius brought through the pool Bobbin's adopted mother and her children, who had been just like a true family to Bobbin. They were now royally received.

There was no happier person in the universe than Bobbin. During the speeches the bamfoon sat enthralled by all the people who spoke. The Wizard of Horgan could hardly contain himself, until at last he was allowed to give a lengthy speech, while everybody began to yawn. All except bamfoon, over whom the Wizard of Horgan seemed to have a hypnotic hold.

The feast and celebrations went on throughout the night. It was the best day of Bobbin's life.

REWARDS AND BLESSINGS

His quest complete Bobbin was now ready to embark on a new adventure. Both grandfathers, together with his parents, had started to plan the best future for Bobbin. The greatest teachers were chosen to ensure that he would gain wisdom and knowledge.

Meanwhile the large hall of the palace was filled with people and friends from all over the world. Oceanius was certain to bless his family with many rewards. There were titles and honours to be bestowed, the details of which only Oceanius knew. A sense of wonder fell on everyone as they waited.

Oceanius began by giving Sealron and Airiel the kingdom of Marine Controlus to look after. From there Sealron would govern many parts of the earth and seas. Next, Maera was made not only a Princess of the sea but also a royal princess of Delphinia. She was chosen to rule Delphinia as queen after her grandfather the king, and would go to Delphinia straight away to begin training in government. This pleased her grandfather because he knew that she would make a good ruler one day.

Monkey was given a special gift from Oceanius. He was given the power of speech. Monkey was already a wise creature. Now with the gift of speech he could be an aid to Bobbin.

Bamfoon could not believe he was to receive a gift, but when it came, his was the power to return to Horgan at any time he desired, accompanied by Casana. The Sea-god gave him a little box which, each time he shook it, would enable him to come from the Isle of Bamfoon to Horgan or vice versa. The bamfoon shook with delight. He really loved the Island of Horgan.

The Wizard of Horgan received the fine gift of Freeman of the South Seas. This pleased him mightily. He was about to reply with a great speech when Oceanius stopped him quickly in his tracks, saying politely that there was no time for a speech presently because so many blessings were still to be given out.

All Bobbin's friends received some honour, before the final one was handed out to him.

Oceanius began, 'Bobbin, because you are still very young, and have such need to learn and be taught so much...

'All too soon you will be a man and you will need to be trained to cope with the government I have in mind for you. Therefore I have decided, along with your parents and the King of Delphinia, that it would be in your best interests if we continue your education in the arts of magic, in which you may gain much useful knowledge.

'You will study for seven years, by which time you will be twenty-one, and ready to accept responsiblity in the Council of the Seas and Lands. Until that time I have decreed that you will spend a year of training with the following people:

'Your first year will be spent under the direction of Gwillum, who will teach you many arts, amongst them knotting and bone reading.

'The second year will be with your friend, King Jack, and with him you will come to understand such arts as friendship and the skill of bowmanship.

'During the third year you will go with Tryeena, the witch of Gumboria, who knows both the arts of the black and the white magic.

'Your old friend, the Wizard of Horgan, will take you for the fourth year, to teach you the art of talking and understanding from listening...' Bobbin smiled, but thought apprehensively of what a very boring time that was going to be.

The Wizard of Horgan could not contain himself, 'Oh, I shall look forward to that so much! There are so many things that I would like to tell you! And—'

'In your fifth year the Green man will teach you how to perform Positive-thinking in the Patterns of Vexor, and the Sea-Oracle will teach you during your sixth year how to gaze into the pools of wisdom, as well as showing you how to look into people's minds.

'Finally, the important seventh year of studies will be directed toward an overall review of what all the others have taught you. It will be a refresher course. On completion of the seventh year you will receive a diploma from the greatest member of the magic circle, who works directly under me. His service is invaluable. He is Noguila. He is the Wisest Wizard in Wizardom.'

Bobbin stood silent. What a task lay ahead of him! Seven long years to study under the world's best teachers. Each one of his tutors was so different.

'Do you accept, Bobbin? Will you be obedient to your trainers and do all they ask you to do?' boomed out the voice of the mighty Oceanius, above the noise of the crowd.

'Yes, Sire, I will obey the rules of my trainers.'

'That is good, and I am pleased with you, Bobbin.'

'Sire, may I ask one question?'

'You may do so.'

'Then may I be allowed to keep wearing these clothes that I feel most comfortable in? You see, when I'm in the sea I can swim about well in them, and when I come out of water — well — they just dry on me.'

The King laughed loudly. 'Believe me, Bobbin, those clothes you have on are past their time now, although they have served their purpose well. But, I shall now give you a new suit of clothes that will also be so comfortable that that you will not want to take them off.

'For, as you shall see presently, I am now giving you a pair of long trousers that will grow along with your stature. The shirt will do the same. There is magic in them. They will change their colours to match your surroundings. When your training is over, Bobbin, there will be a wardrobe of special clothes waiting for you.'

The clothes were brought to Bobbin, who went away to change into them. Feeling comfortable in them he stood once more before Oceanius. Bobbin was very happy.

'Now, Bobbin, leave immediately. You will be under the supervision of Gwillum, who shall instruct you and give you assignments that must be completed. Go now, with my blessing, and do well!'

Bobbin said goodbye to everyone and walked away with Gwillum. He knew that King Jack had trained under Gwillum, who had the power to defeat Death. Bobbin bade farewell to all, without sorrow, for they all saw that he had left to start his new life.